# Snakehead Invasion
## *An Up North Adventure*

D1515885

# Snakehead Invasion
## *An Up North Adventure*

G. M. Moore

# Snakehead Invasion
## An Up North Adventure

ISBN: 978-1475005219

Printed in the United States of America

For my mother, Nancy,
and my sisters, Kimberly and Angela.

*Thank you.*

# FRANKENFISH
# UNLEASHED

The order called for eight-inch suckers—fifteen dozen to be exact. George Dooley smiled, pressed his palms together, and looked up. *Thank you, Happy Hooker.* The bait and tackle store's order was a savior, to be sure. That seemed to be how it worked these days. Just when his money ran out, the good Lord came through with an order. George shook his head with amazement and stepped outside his battered ten-foot caravan trailer and into the early morning fog. He shivered against the cool October air as he made his way to an old barn nestled snugly into the surrounding woods. The converted barn housed a small fishery that was to have helped George and Marge Dooley finance their retirement dream of building a lakeside cabin in the north woods of Wisconsin.

But that was before Marge got sick.

Now, the wood frame of their dream sat rotting near the banks of Spider Lake. For George, the dream had died when Marge did, not that he had the money to finish the cabin, anyway. Their retirement money had been eaten up by hospital bills and funeral costs. What he had left and what he made raising minnows and suckerfish barely paid the taxes on the waterfront property. After a lifetime of hard work, the land, the trailer, and the barn were all that seventy-three-year-old George Dooley had.

The sound of bubbling water filled the dimly lit barn as George walked among the rows of rusty metal tanks. He needed to get the order filled and delivered before The Happy Hooker opened at 7:00 AM. It was now 5:45. He wheeled a large bucket over to one of the tanks, grabbed a hose, and filled the bucket with water. Net in hand, he bent over the tank, but then he quickly pulled back. His face contorted with confusion. "What the heck?" George jerked the cord of an overhead light, and the fluorescent bulb sputtered on. What he saw made him gasp. The water's surface was bloodied with mutilated fish. The suckers in this tank had been attacked—but by what? *A raccoon?* he wondered. George scanned the room but saw nothing. He got a flashlight and searched the barn. Still he found nothing. He went back to the tank and shined the flashlight into its bubbling four-foot-deep water. Dozens of fish swam serenely around the tank. Nothing was out of the norm there. But as George pulled the flashlight back, the tank exploded with movement. Fish darted frantically around. Some bolted to the surface. Others dove deeper. A skinny eel-like fish lunged forward and with vicious zeal caught a sucker by the tail fin. It whipped its prey back and forth so violently that the sucker's tail ripped off. Then the attacker disappeared into the depths of the tank as quickly as it had emerged.

Stunned, George watched the tailless fish struggling to swim.

Lines of blood streamed from its shredded body as it rolled sideways again and again, until it finally stopped struggling and drifted, lifeless, to the surface.

*That eel-like fish has to be a bowfin,* George thought. He grabbed the tally sheet attached to the side of the tank. *Yep, here it is, written plain as day.* He had put two bowfin fish in the tank about a month ago. Still puzzled, he stared at the mangled suckers while he thought. *Bowfins are predators.* He knew that. But the bowfins in this tank were young and well fed. *There shouldn't have been a problem here,* he mused. *Young bowfins eat insects and plankton, not other fish. They shouldn't attack like that.* George rubbed the whisker stubble on his chin back and forth.

But they had.

He had to get those bowfins out of that tank, pronto!

George Dooley scratched the back of his leg as he peered out the small trailer window on a January afternoon. The snowdrifts outside climbed steadily upward. *Soon I'll be living in an igloo,* he thought, and he continued scratching. His wool underwear itched something awful, but George had learned to tolerate it. Itching was better than freezing, and Wisconsin winters were brutal. The wood-burning stove he had installed that very first winter without Marge provided the trailer's only heat. He turned to shoo a calico cat out of a recliner positioned near the stove and sat down himself. The cat hissed softly and quickly jumped onto George's lap. He pushed her back to the floor. The cat hissed again.

"Leave me be, Callie," George ordered. "My trailer. My chair."

Callie reluctantly turned away and nestled into a spot on the nearby sofa. George leaned back, and the recliner's footrest popped out. "Ahhhhhhhhh," he sighed. With his greasy salt-and-pepper hair slicked back and hands resting on his round belly, he smiled smugly at the cat. Callie stared at him and then turned her head away. "Sore loser," he huffed.

A loud bark suddenly sounded from outside the front door. George let out an annoyed growl. "I can't get a moment's peace around here." He pushed the footrest back down and went to the door, just as the bark rang out again.

"Oh, hold your horses. I'm comin'."

George held the door open, and a black-and-tan hound leaped into the trailer. The dog headed for the sofa. "Oh no, you don't, Ace. Get back here." Ace hesitated and then turned his head to look at George. "Get over here," the man ordered. Ace hung his head and reluctantly followed the command. George filled a bucket with warm water and dipped Ace's snow-packed paws in, one at a time. He grabbed a towel and dried each paw before releasing the dog with, "You're done." Ace flew to the sofa and snuggled in on the side farthest away from the cat.

George smiled sympathetically at the two animals. He had found Callie about three years ago, bloody, at the side of the highway. Whatever had hit her had torn off her tail, ripped off an ear, and broken her back leg. He had found Ace on a trip to the old dump a year or so later. The poor dog only had one eye and had been left for dead in a heap of garbage. George wasn't sure why he had brought the animals home or why he had nursed them back to health. A project to occupy his time, he guessed. He also wasn't sure why he kept them or why they stayed. But here they all were.

"A bunch of rejects, we are," he chuckled and shook his head.

Before he sat back down, George decided to put another log on the fire. But when he went to the woodpile stacked just off the kitchen, he found it gone. *That's just great,* he grumbled to himself. *Never a moment's peace around here!* George threw on his coat, stepped into his snow boots, and headed for the barn. He needed to buy a cord of wood in town, but there was no need to make a special trip. He went into Minong on Saturdays, weather permitting. That was his bath day. The trailer's restroom held only a small sink and toilet, so spring through fall, George suited up and bathed in the lake. But in the winter, he gave himself the luxury of a hot shower at the YMCA. To hold him over until he could buy the wood on Saturday, George had cut down a small spruce earlier in the week, and to keep the wood dry, he had dragged it into the barn's storage area. Now he simply took a chainsaw and cut pieces as he needed them.

Once in the barn, George removed his wet boots. The last thing he needed at his age was to slip and fall on the icy-cold cement floor. But still, on his way to the storage area, his foot landed in a puddle of freezing water. "Dagnabbit!" he yelled and jerked his now-soaked sock off the floor. George grabbed the side of a large glass tank to steady himself and immediately saw the source of the puddle. The glass tank was cracked as if someone had hit it with a baseball. Water dripped from spidery veins in the panel. George felt the area with his hand and then walked around the tank, examining it from every side. *Strange,* he thought. The glass bulged outward, not inward. Something had hit the glass from the *inside.* George stared suspiciously at the four eel-like fish hovering, unmoving, in the water. *No,* he thought. *Not possible.*

George bent down to get a better look at the splintered glass, and one of the fish suddenly sprang to life. With one quick thrust, it lunged head first at George and crashed into the glass before him. George jumped back. He slipped on the frozen ground and fell hard. A strange popping sound echoed from his wrist as he landed.

"Crazy fish!" he roared and cradled his injured arm. He stared up at the tank in angry confusion. *Those fish are not bowfin. They can't be—but they look just like them.* His mind searched for a clue. They were tubular in shape, were brownish olive with dark blotches, and had a long, single dorsal fin—exactly how you would describe a bowfin. *And the teeth.* George's mind suddenly rang with alarm. Bowfin carried the nickname "dogfish" because of their strong, sharp teeth. These fish had those same flesh-tearing teeth. But these creatures were way more aggressive—way more dangerous.

*These fish are loco,* his mind cried. *They're like monsters. They're ... they're ... they're Frankenfish!*

George had been given four of these eel-like creatures to raise until spring. They had started as small fry, but now two had grown to about eight inches long and two to about ten inches. After the sucker incident, George had moved the two smaller fish into the glass tank with the larger ones. He kept these glass tanks more for show than anything else. People liked watching the fish swim around, and so did he. He especially liked keeping an eye on these strange fish. *They're like pit bulls with fins,* he thought as he struggled to his feet. *Maybe I'm raising some type of hybrid or mixed breed—but for what purpose?*

Whatever they were, he was going to have to move them—again. He gently rubbed his swelling, throbbing wrist. He sighed with frustration. *Looks like I'll be going into town early after all.* George glared into the glass tank.

"But don't worry," he said out loud. "I'll deal with you four first."

✳ ✳ ✳ ✳

Crisp March air blew through George Dooley's barn as the CD player cranked out Johnny Horton's greatest hits. George sang along with the old country crooner as he worked in the fishery, feeding dried worms to the minnows.

*"As I walked in the door, the music was clear. The purtiest voice I had heard in two years. The song she was singin' made a man's blood run cold. When it's springtime in Alaska, it's forty below."*

He loved that song. Even though it wasn't forty below, it was springtime in Wisconsin, and the ruggedness of that song reminded George of life in the north woods.

If George lived for anything these days, it was for spring. Crappie season was just around the corner. As fishing picked up, his cabin fever packed up. Spring brought with it a twenty-degree jump in temperature. It was about fifty degrees outside, and George had the barn's double door open. The fresh air pouring in was wonderful. Callie and Ace milled about. The sun was shining. It was a wonderful day.

*"I reached for the gal who was singin' the tune. We did the Eskeemo Hop all around the sea-loon."*

George continued his happy duet with Johnny Horton—until a low, guttural hiss broke through the music. He lowered the volume on the CD player and quietly listened. He heard the hiss again. It was Callie. She roared defensively and then fell silent.

Suddenly, the cat's tortured shriek filled the barn. George dropped the worm container and ran toward the sound.

He was shocked to find Callie crouched low and hissing as she circled three eel-like fish slithering on the cement floor. For a moment, George couldn't move. All he could do was stare at the slithering fish and at Callie hobbling on a bloody paw. Slowly, George turned his head toward a nearby tank. There, the fourth fish hurled itself repeatedly at a shredded hole in the tank's steel mesh cover. Those Frankenfish had escaped by gnawing through steel and flinging themselves out of the tank. *Unbelievable.* George looked back to the three fish on the floor. *And they bit a cat.*

"They bit a cat," he repeated out loud, as if trying to make the fact sink in.

Wild barking shook George from his trance. Ace had finally gotten to the scene and wasn't happy with what he'd found.

"Back!" George commanded. "Back!" He was being paid fifty dollars a week to keep these fish alive and well. Frankenfish or not, he was protecting his investment. He needed the money.

"Back! Sit!" George waved his hand downward as Ace reluctantly stepped back and sat. George scooped Callie off the floor and scratched her soothingly behind the one ear she had left. "Good girl, Callie." He carefully placed the cat behind Ace. "You stay there," he ordered. She looked up at him with frightened, saucer-like eyes. "It's okay," he assured her. "You did good."

When George turned back, the fourth fish had finally gotten itself through the steel mesh and was struggling on the tank's rim—half in, half out of the water. He used his fist to pound it back into the tank; then he walked toward the fish still making their slow escape across the floor.

"Don't know where you think you're going, but if any of you

bite me, there's going to be a fish fry tonight. Fifty dollars or no fifty dollars, you're all frying."

It was now late May, and George welcomed the summer tourism season with open arms. He heard a car pull up, and a smile quickly spread across his face. *Finally.* He had kept those crazy Frankenfish a month longer than he'd expected, and now that there was more business to be had, he was ready to be rid of them. George headed to the barn and waited there as the Department of Natural Resources ranger exited the SUV. "Come on in," he said as he waved her in the door. "They're all ready for you. I can say I'll be glad to see them gone."

"I paid you well to keep them," she said flatly.

Her tone took him aback. She was usually very friendly. George simply nodded and motioned toward a container sitting on the floor. "You be careful with that. I put them in a special sealed container for you. They're vicious things. You won't believe what—"

She cut him off with a curt, "It's fine. Thanks."

George eyed her curiously. She was acting strangely. He forced a small smile and continued on. "They're not bowfins, are they? They don't act like bowfins. Do you know how aggressive they are?" She stared at him. "Of course you do. Well, what are they?"

"That's not your concern," she answered and grabbed the container's handles. As she carried the fish to her SUV, George followed.

"Are they a hybrid fish? An experiment?"

She didn't answer, just got in the vehicle and started up the engine. George leaned in the open window. "Well, what on earth are you going to do with them?"

"It's not your business, George." She gave him a reluctant smile. "Thank you for your help." Then she backed up the vehicle.

George stepped away and watched her leave. His brow furrowed. *Something's not right here*, he thought. He turned and walked to the back of the barn, where a pile of boxes and packaging had been accumulating since winter. He needed to make a trip to the dump and soon, he thought, as he sorted through the soggy rubble. *Ah, there it is.* He pulled out a cardboard container dotted with holes on both sides. He examined the warped, peeling box and started removing layers of tape crisscrossing the sides. *Aha.* Someone had gone to great effort to conceal the original address label. The label's edges were frayed, as if someone had tried to peel it off, but then the address had been marked out and covered with tape instead. Wisconsin's freeze-and-thaw cycle had worked its magic, though, and George easily removed the label. He held it up to the sun and read through its backside. He made out:

E. P_ _ts
22 _ _ S. W_nt_or_h
Chi_ _g_ _ _ L 60_ _ _

*South Wentworth in Chicago?* George had been born and raised in Chicago. He knew that address. It was Chinatown. *Why would someone ship fish from Chinatown to Wisconsin?* It didn't make sense. *This isn't right*, he thought again. Whatever was going on, he was now a part of it, and he didn't like that one bit.

George took the container and the label into his trailer for safekeeping. *Just in case ...*

# North to Wisconsin

*Where is it?*

Corbett Griffith III rummaged through his dresser drawers, tossing clothes out and over his shoulder to the floor.

"Mom! Mom!" he bellowed as he pulled open yet another drawer. "Mom!"

*She's always messing with my stuff,* he grumbled to himself. *Always cleaning and moving things around.* "Can never find anything I want," he huffed out loud. Pushing his shaggy dark-brown hair off his face, he stood up, turned around, and froze. There she was standing quietly in the doorway. He gulped slightly. She always did that, too—just appeared like that, out of nowhere.

"Yes?" his mother asked.

Corbett quickly pulled himself together. He glared at his

mother and, with an accusatory tone, asked, "Where's my mosquito bandana? I can't find it anywhere."

His mom calmly walked over to one of the open drawers, reached in, and pulled out a black bandana decorated with white mosquitoes. She handed it to Corbett without saying a word.

"I *looked* in there," he whined.

"Try looking with your eyes and not with your mouth. It helps."

She moved to Corbett's bed. He dove to block her but wasn't quick enough.

"Come on, Mom. You can check it all out later."

"Packing a little early, aren't you?" she asked as she sorted through the bags covering the bed. "Four pairs of underwear? For two months?" she questioned skeptically.

Corbett shrugged. He was way too excited to sweat the small stuff like counting underwear. He had been packing all afternoon for his annual summer trip to Uncle Dell's Whispering Pines Lodge. Focus was a little hard to achieve right now, because just yesterday his dad had promised to come up to Wisconsin for a week. The two of them would be hanging out and having fun together for a whole week. Corbett couldn't wait, but still, at age twelve, he was no dummy. He figured his dad's promise had a lot more to do with his mom than with him. Corbett's mom had spent almost a month at Whispering Pines after the Sleepy Eye Elk discovery the summer before. *That gave Dad some big-time guilt*, he thought. And then there was Rick, his mom's boyfriend. Corbett was pretty sure his dad's sudden interest in him and Wisconsin had something to do with Rick, as well. Fear? Jealousy? More guilt? Corbett didn't know and really didn't care. His dad had promised to spend a week with him. The *why* was small stuff, and he wasn't going to sweat it.

"You need more than four pairs of underwear," his mother was lecturing. "And something warmer than shorts and T-shirts."

"Okay, okay."

"What about a swimsuit? I don't see a swimsuit."

Corbett nodded repeatedly and waved his mother toward the door. "I've got this. You can check it later."

Still, she lingered in his room. "Corbett," she started, then paused and gave him a half smile. "You really shouldn't get your hopes up about your dad. You know? He might not make it up. He's got a lot going on."

"He's going to come, Mom. He promised."

"Yes, but backing out isn't out of the norm for him. You know that."

Corbett returned his mom's half smile but didn't say anything. Awkward silence followed.

"All right," she finally said. "Rick is on standby, just in case. You know, he's a teacher and has the same time off you do. He'd love to see the lodge and get to know you better."

Corbett still didn't say anything. He just stood there with that half smile locked on his face. He didn't want Rick anywhere near Whispering Pines Lodge. The guy seemed all right, but Corbett really wished Rick would stop bothering him—and them. Stop trying to play Wii. Stop offering to play catch. Stop showing up everywhere! Everything about the guy annoyed Corbett, even his looks. *Those wimpy wire-framed glasses,* Corbett smirked, *and that neat little mustache and beard makes the guy look like such a geek.* What Corbett really, really wished was that his mom would see the light and not actually want to *marry* the guy. *Just dump the nerdy dude.* They didn't need Rick around. For Corbett, a stepdad was not part of the picture—here in Chicago or up in Wisconsin.

His mom sighed sadly as she turned toward the door. "Well, keep an open mind about it."

Corbett slowly nodded as he watched her step through the doorway and into the hall. The only thing he was keeping an open mind about these days was the Whispering Pines fish house. Scalers, skinners, and knives: he shuddered at the thought of using those torture tools, but his resolve was set. He was going to learn how to clean a fish this year, period. He was going to learn how to fillet *and* run the motor on the dinghy his uncle had christened *The Lucky 13.* Corbett's best friend, Pike, who was a year older and had grown up on the lakes of northern Wisconsin, would be his guide and instructor. During the summer, he and Pike helped Uncle Dell run Whispering Pines Lodge, but they always had plenty of free time. The boys had mapped everything out over e-mail. Corbett chuckled. Minong was finally catching up with the rest of the world. The Internet had arrived—at least to Pike's family at The Happy Hooker. Now he and Pike could easily stay in touch and plot their next adventure. For Corbett, that would be mastering everything about fishing and boating before his dad arrived at Whispering Pines. Corbett really wanted to impress him. Sure, he had caught a ferocious world record muskie and had discovered a ten-thousand-year-old elk skeleton—but his dad hadn't been around to see either one of those achievements. He hadn't witnessed them firsthand. This was the year, definitely the year. A smile spread across Corbett's face as he hurriedly began packing again. He heard an alert sound on his computer, shoved some jeans into a bag, and raced to the screen. He had mail. It read:

> *Get up here, Grif. Bored. Good Gouda, fishing stinks!*
> *How soon can you come? Pike*

Corbett's smile got even bigger. Seeing his nickname in print and Pike's odd habit of using cheese for curse words always did that. He couldn't wait to leave "Corbett" behind in Chicago and become "Griffy" again. Maybe he could leave early. School was out in a week. Nothing was keeping him here.

*Stand by,* he quickly typed and bolted to the doorway.

"Hey, Mom!" he yelled down the hall. No answer. *She's never around when I really need her. Jeez!* "Mom!" he yelled again and kept yelling as he ran down the stairs to find her.

# SPIDER LAKE RISING

The motorboat glided along the shoreline of Lost Land Lake, as the sun cast its final orange glow across the water. Fish twisted angrily in a sealed container at the driver's feet.

"Calm down," she whispered soothingly. "It's almost time."

Her face darkened as she approached a pontoon filled with vacationers. The boat carried the Sleepy Eye Rentals logo. *Tourist trap*, she thought, scowling, but then quickly forced a smile and waved happily to its passengers as she passed. *Nothing going on here, folks. Just keep on fishing.*

At Sunken Island Resort, she cut the motor and let the boat glide to a stop. The water was calm tonight. She looked around. A few other boats were in sight, but none too close, and nobody was on shore. *Perfect.*

She kept the container hidden on the bottom of the boat. Not wanting to attract any unnecessary attention, she hunched over and slowly opened the lid. Squinting against the water that splashed out, she plunged her arm in. The fish slipped and flipped out of her grasp again and again. "Hold still!" she ordered just as a set of teeth closed sharply on her forearm. Gulping back pain, she pulled her arm out and slammed the lid shut. Beads of blood popped up in a semicircular pattern across her arm. As she watched the red beads slowly ooze together, her resolve wavered. *Is this really the answer?* she asked herself. *Is this the right move? These fish are vicious and could ruin Lost Land Lake. Can I live with that?* A headline she had read not long ago popped into her head: "Snakehead Invasion Prompts Officials to Poison Pond." Soon that would be the fate of Lost Land Lake. No world record muskie or ancient elk discovery could save the lake then. She imagined a day when her Spider Lake was the number-one tourist draw, when her Empire Lodge buzzed with activity, when her bills were being paid. She grinned. *No more Lost Land Lake this, Lost Land Lake that. And, yes, I can live with that.*

Thump! Thump! Thump!

The sound of angry snakeheads thrashing inside the container drew her back to the task at hand. She cleared her mind and dismissed the doubt with one shake of her head. Okay, she'd have to risk a different approach. She looked around again. It was still clear. She picked up the container, tilted it over the boat's side, and slowly opened the lid—just a crack. She gave the container a shake. One fish slid out and into the water. She shook it again. The second fish followed. She quickly closed the lid and set the container down.

*Two down. Two to go.*

Tucking in a few loose strands of dark-blonde hair, she adjusted the DNR cap on her head, cranked up the motor, and turned the boat toward Whispering Pines Bay.

# A FEW GOOD
# LESSONS

Thanks to some heavy persuading, Griffy found himself up north a whole two weeks earlier than normal. As soon as school let out for summer break, his mom had him loaded up and on the road to Wisconsin. The long car ride from Chicago was not so grueling this year. Griffy knew the curves and hills of County A highway very well by now and didn't get carsick once. He didn't even have to look for Whispering Pines among the sea of arrows at the head of each fork in the road. Uncle Dell tested him at every intersection, asking "Which way?" and Griffy would quickly call out, "Take a left" or "Take the right." He proudly got the answer correct each time.

So now here he was, just a few days later, weaving in and out of the spruce, pine, and birch trees that dotted the grounds of Whispering Pines Lodge. The scent of pine filled the warm

June air, and Griffy took in a deep breath of it. That smell always reminded him of Wisconsin. Even at Christmas, the smell of pine garland brought him back to the sloping peninsula that Whispering Pines called home. Dry pine needles crunched under his feet. He was savoring the sound and in no hurry, but they were waiting for him.

"Hurry it up, Grif!" Pike called from outside the fish house.

Griffy passed one brown clapboard cabin and then another, as he made his way down to the swim bay. He saw that Uncle Dell was already in the fish house. *Great,* Griffy silently huffed. He wasn't sure he was ready for this. Not sure at all.

"Sweet Brie, why are you being so slow?" Pike called out again, in obvious agony.

Griffy broke into a slow trot, and before he knew it, Spinner was trotting at his side. The dog always seemed to appear out of nowhere. Spinner looked up at Griffy, his white, bushy eyebrows raised against his black, wavy fur, as if he were asking a question: *Hey, what's going on? Where you going?*

"Just headed to the fish house to learn to fillet."

Griffy had been up the hill at Cabin 12, closing a vent and installing a screen on its stone fireplace. A bat had found its way down the chimney and into the cabin the night before. He chuckled as he remembered the chaos the Donovans had created when they'd bolted from the cabin in hysterics. They'd awakened the entire resort with their screams. Mr. Donovan had showed up at the lodge barefoot and wearing what looked like nothing but a bathrobe. Something was in the cabin, he'd said. They didn't know what, but it had attacked the entire family. Griffy stifled a snort as he pictured Mrs. Donovan standing among the trees in her pajamas, hair pulled back, gooey cream all over her face, and a piece of tape stuck to her upper lip. The scene that followed was made for YouTube: five men, his uncle included, chasing a crazed bat around with fishing nets. It had taken more than an hour, but Uncle Dell had finally netted the poor creature and released it safely outside.

Still smirking over the late-night mishap, Griffy trotted up to Pike. "Okay, I'm here," he announced. Spinner busied himself sniffing the ground.

"'Bout time," Pike replied and quickly ran to the fish house door. He pushed his face against the screen. His unruly sandy-blond hair poked through the holes as he whispered something to Uncle Dell. Dell whispered back, opened the door a crack, and passed something to Pike.

"What's going on?" Griffy asked suspiciously.

Pike walked toward him with the something hidden behind his back. A huge smile covered his face and his brown eyes had a glint in them that Griffy knew meant trouble. He took a step back. He watched his uncle leave the fish house and follow behind Pike. He was smiling, too.

"What?" Griffy asked again. "What are you guys up to?"

"Just this," Pike announced as he whipped the object out from behind his back in a ta-da motion.

Griffy looked to his uncle. Dell nodded reassuringly. "Go ahead. Take it. Every good fisherman needs his own knife."

Griffy took the knife from his friend, with a big grin, as he examined its wooden handle and leather sheath.

"Dell paid for it, but I picked it out," Pike proudly said. "Check out the blade. It's the coolest."

Griffy took hold of the handle and slowly pulled the knife from its sheath. His own blue eyes sparkled at the sight of the long, thin, shiny silver blade. "Cool," he said and gave the air a few quick swipes.

"That's not for sword play. It's for cleaning fish," his uncle scolded.

Griffy nodded. He looked to Pike, then to Dell. "This is the best. Thanks," he said, beaming.

"So, you ready?" Uncle Dell asked.

"Of course he is," Pike fired back and headed into the fish house.

Griffy felt his stomach clench, but he nodded enthusiastically. "Yep. Ready."

The fish house really wasn't a place Griffy liked or wanted to be. *Disgusting* was the only word to describe it. It looked disgusting. It smelled disgusting. And with all the flies and mosquitoes buzzing around, it even sounded disgusting. But if he wanted to learn to fillet and impress his dad, that's where he had to be.

Griffy stepped up to the bloodstained countertop and was surprised to find that it hit him just above his belt. He obviously had grown a few inches since last summer. He glanced over at Pike. The older boy was still taller, thinner, and more muscular, but not by much. Griffy grinned smugly as he hung his knife's sheath on a nail and waited for instruction.

"Grab a fish," his uncle said, pointing toward the sink at the end of the counter. Griffy peered into the sink at three bluegill and two rock bass. He hesitated. Pike grunted impatiently, reached over him, got a fish, and placed it on the counter. "Here."

A lump formed in Griffy's throat as he eyed his victim.

"Hold the fish like this, with your palm," Uncle Dell instructed, "and then make a cut across the fish going under the ear flap and pectoral fin."

Griffy watched his uncle closely, then mimicked him by pressing his palm into the bluegill's scaly side. He flinched. *Cold and slimy. Ewwwwwwww.* Griffy could swear he heard the fish gasp, so he lightened his grip. With his face frozen in a grimace, he placed the blade against the fish and guided it gently across. Nothing. He didn't even break the skin. He started over, pressing the blade down harder. The fish slid from under the blade and fell to the floor.

"No, no, no!" his friend ranted as he reached down and snatched the fish off the cement floor. "You've got to really press down *hard*. You can't be wimpy about it." He slapped the bluegill back onto the countertop and slammed his palm down on it. "Like this. See?"

Griffy nodded, waved Pike away, and tried again. This time he held the fish firmly. He turned his head away and closed his eyes as he stabbed the knife in. He watched the knife through a tight squint as it sliced the bluegill's flesh, bracing himself for the gush of blood sure to come. *Wait a minute.* His eyes popped open wide. *No blood—hey, where's the blood?* As he continued slicing through the translucent flesh, only a thin line of red liquid oozed out. *This isn't bad. I can handle this.* The grimace slowly left his face.

"Okay. That's good," Dell said, watching over Griffy's shoulder. "Now, cut along the dorsal fin; at the end of the fin, push the blade through to the other side. Angle the blade like this, and slice down to the tail fin."

With Pike watching on one side and Dell on the other, Griffy completed each step easily. He looked up at Dell for approval. His uncle smiled. "That's it. Now, cut farther in along the dorsal side. All right. Keep cutting until you find the rib cage."

Griffy pulled the flap of meat and skin back. He could see bones and spidery black veins running through the fish's body.

"There it is." Pike pointed over his friend's shoulder. "That's the rib cage. See it?"

Griffy did. He sliced up and over the rib cage and continued cutting until the bluegill's entire right side was removed.

"Just take off the skin, and you're done," Pike said as he wiped his hands together.

"With side one," Dell countered.

Griffy removed the skin and held up his first fillet for all to see. He wasn't too impressed. All that work for one little piece of ragged meat? It hardly seemed worth the trouble.

"Not bad," Pike encouraged. "I've seen worse from my sister."

"Yep, not bad for the first try," Uncle Dell agreed. "Side two will be better. Promise."

"If you say so," Griffy replied sullenly and flipped the fish over.

By the third fish Griffy was better and faster. His fillets weren't so ragged looking; they were still not as good as Uncle Dell's, but they were getting there. Pleased with his nephew's progress, Dell left the boys in the fish house to finish up. Pike chased and swatted flies, while Griffy prepared to fillet the last practice fish. As he pressed his palm down on the rock bass, a stream of pee shot out of the fish right at him. Griffy flinched and jumped back. He slammed into Pike and lost his grip on the fillet knife. Griffy watched in what seemed like slow motion as the knife flipped over and over on its way to the ground. He braced for the painful impact as the blade landed solidly, point first, in his foot. He cried out, then looked down in confusion. *It didn't hurt. Why didn't it hurt?* he wondered. There the knife was, stuck in the flesh between his big toe and second toe. *But wait. That's a sandal. I am wearing sneakers.*

"Good Gouda! Gouda! Gouda! Gouda!" came a distressing cry behind him.

*Oh no! That's Pike's foot, not mine.* Griffy turned and got a good look at his friend. The world quickly went from slow motion to fast forward. Griffy didn't know what to do first. Get Uncle Dell? Get a first-aid kit? A bandage?

"Pull it out! Pull it out!" Pike yelled as he fell back against the wall. Color drained from his face.

Griffy didn't think twice. He just pulled. His eyes widened in shock, as blood gushed from the open wound. *There's the blood,* he thought and watched Pike slump to the floor.

"Uncle Dell!" Griffy yelled in panic. He opened the screen door to yell again but saw that Spinner was racing down the Whispering Pines beach toward Dell. The dog bit the leg of Dell's pants and pulled. Dell looked over, saw Griffy frantically waving, dropped the rake in his hand, and ran toward his nephew.

Griffy looked down at the now ghost-white Pike. He quickly searched the fish house for something to stop his friend's bleeding, but all the rags and towels hanging around were dirty and covered with fish scales. Pike slowly opened his eyes just a slit, then closed them tight again. "I can't look," he said, wincing. "How bad is it?"

"I don't know. I don't know." Griffy felt like crying. "There's too much blood."

"What?" Pike cried out. His eyes flew open. He saw the blood and moaned, "I'm gonna be sick."

Griffy acted quickly. He hated being shirtless—unless, of

course, he was swimming—but this was an emergency. So, he ripped off his T-shirt, wadded it up, and pressed it firmly on Pike's bloody foot. The screen door sprang open behind him. It was Uncle Dell.

"What happened here?" he demanded through heavy breaths. Dell's hat now sat askew on his graying head of crew-cut hair, and his plaid cotton shirt was half tucked in, half hanging out.

Griffy bit his lower lip and shrugged. "The fillet knife fell," he said guiltily. His stomach heaved as he pulled the bloody T-shirt off Pike's wound. He watched as worry spread across his uncle's face.

"Go call the McKendricks. Tell them to meet us at the emergency room. This looks like stitches to me."

Griffy nodded, and as he shoved open the screen door and bolted out of the fish house, he couldn't help but think, *Good thing my dad wasn't here to see this.*

✳   ✳   ✳   ✳

About four days later, Griffy stood on the shore of Lost Land Lake, throwing rocks into Whispering Pines Bay as he waited for Pike. He hadn't seen his friend since a nurse had pushed Pike out of the Minong Clinic in a wheelchair with three stitches in his foot. Griffy felt awful—still. He had faithfully practiced filleting every day since the accident. He didn't want to be the cause of any more knife injuries, and he really wanted to master the skill before his dad came up. The fish house still grossed him out, but he was slowly getting used to the blood, slime, goo, and occasional squirt of pee that came with cleaning a fish.

"Yo! Grif!"

He turned to see Pike waving and limping his way down the embankment. Griffy quickly ran up to meet him. "Finally, you're out. If your imprisonment had lasted one more day, I would have lost it—completely!"

"You?" Pike questioned. "What about me? I've been trapped behind the counter at The Happy Hooker. With Gil! It was torture."

Griffy nodded sympathetically. Pike's sister, Gil, was sixteen now, had her driver's license, and thought she was hot stuff. Since Pike was supposed to stay off his foot for three days, his mom had refused to let him out of the bait and tackle shop or out of her sight. She knew her son too well.

"How's the foot?" Griffy looked down at the fabric bootie secured with Velcro around Pike's right foot. "I'm really, really sorry." He cringed slightly. "But no one told me about the pee. I mean, it shoots right out of 'em."

Pike snickered. "I know. I know. It's so random. You can actually use bluegill as little pee squirt guns. Cracks me up every time." Pike paused and tapped his right leg. "You know this is the same leg the muskie bit?" Griffy hadn't thought about that. Pike pulled up his shorts to show off the scar. "I think I'm going give the muskie credit for this injury, too. Makes a better story, you know?" He eyed Griffy mischievously. "Not only did the muskie bite my leg and drag me down to die, it also tried to bite all my toes off. What do you think?"

"Good Gouda," Griffy sighed and rolled his eyes. He saw Pike's mouth drop from a smile into a pout. "No, it's good," he quickly corrected himself. "Really. Might need a little work, but it's good."

The two boys laughed and joked as they continued down the

embankment and stopped at the shore in front of *The Lucky 13,* Uncle Dell's white-and-red wooden dinghy.

"So, you ready for another lesson?" Pike asked.

"I think the question is, are you ready to give me another lesson?" Griffy nodded toward the bootie-clad foot.

"No worries, dude. Boot comes off in a couple of days; then I'm as good as new. Besides," Pike sneered, "according to my mom, my dad, and Dell, it's my own fault. I should know better than to wear sandals in the fish house. But I had been raking up the swim area, ya know?" He threw his hands up in the air. "Jeez! You don't wear shoes to do that."

Griffy nodded. "I hear ya." He understood very well how unfair adults could be, but he couldn't figure out how Pike had talked his mom into this one. Being thirteen and already experienced, Pike was here to teach him how to operate the dinghy's small motor. Griffy figured that after four days of sulking and moaning and groaning around The Happy Hooker, his friend had probably just worn his mother down. Uncle Dell likely helped the cause, too. He had assured Pike's mom that captaining the small wooden boat was no big deal. It only had a four-horsepower motor, after all. The boys could handle it. Many lawnmowers had more power than that.

"It's all good," Pike assured. "My only instructions were not to get my foot wet. So, I'll get in, and you push us off."

Griffy unwrapped *The Lucky 13*'s anchor from around a nearby tree, placed it in the boat, and got his own feet wet as he pushed the boat away from shore and then hopped in.

"I'll take us out a bit," Pike said as he grabbed the oars and started rowing. "We'll need some room and some time. The waves will keep bringing us in, and the motor can be a little touchy."

When they were about twenty-five feet from shore, Griffy moved to the boat's stern and sat in front of the motor. He absently rubbed his own muskie battle scar, as he stared warily at the motor before him. Rubbing the scar on his left arm always made him feel better. But was he ready for this? He felt a little jittery. He blew out a big puff of air. He needed to man up if he was going to really impress his dad. *I can do this. Gil can do it. Pike can do it. I can do it.*

"This is going to be easy-peasy. You'll see. I learned real quick." And with that statement, Pike began the lesson.

"First, open the tank vent. Make sure the motor is in neutral. There are three gears: neutral, forward, and reverse. Set the choke between half and full. Put the throttle in the start position. Prime the tank by squeezing this." Pike held up a black bulb attached to the end of the gas line. "And then pull the starter cord. When the motor fires, adjust the choke and throttle down into a slow idle, like this." Pike pretended to move the choke lever inward and pointed to the rotating part of the motor handle. "To steer," he continued and grabbed the handle, "pull toward you to go left and push away to go right. Twist the handle toward you to go faster. Twist it away to go slower. Got it?"

Griffy stared at the motor, slack jawed, as the boat rocked slowly back and forth in the water. Pike had lost him at 'First, open the tank vent.'

"Got it?" Pike asked again.

"Uh, no," Griffy replied sarcastically. "What exactly is so easy-peasy about that? I have no idea what anything you just said means."

"Oh, come on. It's just like starting a lawnmower. No biggie."

"I've never started a lawnmower."

"What?" Pike questioned sharply.

"We don't have grass."

Pike shot him an incredulous look. "What do you mean, you don't have grass? Who doesn't have grass?"

"I live in a high-rise condo building. We don't have grass," Griffy stated firmly. "And in case you didn't notice, there's not a lot of grass around here, either. A lot of sand and pine needles. Not much grass."

"All right. All right." Pike held up his hands in defeat. "I'll start over and go slow, city boy." He snickered and nudged his friend.

"Ha, ha," Griffy smirked. "Very funny."

Pike repeated all the steps, giving a detailed explanation for each, and then walked Griffy slowly through the process. When it was time to pull the starter cord, Griffy pulled, but nothing happened. He pulled again. Nothing.

"Sometimes it helps to stand and straddle the thing," Pike suggested.

Griffy stood and pulled back hard. Nothing.

"Sometimes you have to adjust the choke." Pike reached over and pushed the choke in. "Try it now, and give it a nice, hard jerk at the end."

Griffy's arm already hurt. He wasn't so sure he had another pull left in him. He took in a deep breath, placed one hand on top of the motor for support, pulled the cord, and jerked as hard as he could. The motor roared to life. It vibrated wildly as its propeller spun in the lake water.

Griffy quickly sat down. "What do I do? What do I do?"

"Idle it down. Here." Pike stood, reached over his friend, and grabbed the shaking handle. "There." The motor quieted. "Now, shift the gear to forward. Take the handle and twist it toward you to go."

Griffy grabbed the handle. The vibration was like a shock wave running through his entire body. The shaking started at his hand and seemed to continue down to his toes. How was he supposed to control this?

"Feels funny, huh?" Pike shouted. "All tingly-like."

Griffy nodded. The two did nothing for a moment, Griffy being shaken constantly by the motor, Pike standing and staring down at him. Pike's stare finally turned into a glare. He nodded toward the handle, as if saying, "Go on. Turn it."

Griffy could barely feel his hand or his arm at this point, but he went ahead and twisted the handle all the way toward him. The boat lurched forward, throwing Pike sideways. His hip hit the lip of the boat, and he fell overboard. Griffy panicked and let go of the motor's handle, as the whitewashed boat raced past Pike and toward shore. Griffy didn't know what to do. The shore was coming up quick. He was going to crash!

"Kill it! Kill it!" he heard Pike yell from behind him.

Griffy got up on his knees and stared down at the motor. He saw a red button and quickly pushed it. The motor died, just as the boat slammed into the rocky lake bottom with a crunch. The impact threw Griffy on top of the motor. His thoughts were a jumbled mess. His body shook. All he knew was that Pike had been thrown from the boat. He had to get in the water. He had to get to Pike. His arms and legs felt like Jell-O as he crawled over the boat's red-trimmed side and into the water. He'd meant to land gracefully on his feet but instead sort of belly flopped into the lake. He came up coughing out water.

"What *are* you doing?" Pike asked as he waded over through the knee-deep water, his sandy-blond hair matted around his face in wet clumps. He was laughing and coughing out water, too. "It's not enough that you keep trying to kill me, you've got to try to off yourself, too?"

Griffy pulled himself up out of the water. He was still a little wobbly, and he choked out his words. "I was—coming—to help—you."

Pike smiled ear to ear, as he gave his friend a hand. "I'm okay. That was so cool. Nice job on the kill button. I kinda forgot to tell you about that."

Griffy was bent over, hands on his knees, slowly composing himself. He looked up at Pike and pushed his dripping brown hair out of his eyes. "Yeah, and you told me to turn the handle, but not how far. Details, dude. Details."

"Sorry," Pike shrugged sheepishly. "You don't have to turn it all the way. Just a little."

Griffy slowly stood up. "Figured that one out the hard way, thanks." He started to laugh. Now that the ordeal was over, it was kind of funny and fun. "*The Lucky 13* can really move."

"No kidding. Ready to try it again?"

"What? No way. Not doing that again."

"You got to. Get back on the horse, you know? Besides, I'm not supposed to get wet, remember? We have to stay out here until this bootie dries, or my mom will actually kill me, not just *try*, like you."

"Funny. Again, funny." Griffy tried to make light of the situation, but he felt awful about it. Pike could have really been hurt.

"Listen. I'm serious. You have to try again." Pike's face

furrowed. "If my mom or anyone else sees me like this, I won't see you or Whispering Pines for the rest of the summer."

Griffy suddenly got serious. He knew Pike was right about that one. Without another word, he climbed back into *The Lucky 13*. Pike followed and gave Griffy step-by-step detailed instructions on starting the motor—again. When it was time for Griffy to pull the cord, the motor fired up on his first try. Pike beamed.

"Out into the bay, Captain," he ordered and gripped the edge of his seat. "But not so fast this time."

Griffy made a face at him. *I can do this*, he assured himself. As his body vibrated with the motor in neutral, he moved the gear to forward and slowly turned the handle toward him. *The Lucky 13* glided through the water. This time, Griffy beamed. *Easy-peasy.*

"Whoopeeee!" Pike cried out and high-fived his friend.

"Woooohoooo!" Griffy joined in the cheer, and the two boys whooped and hollered out into Whispering Pine Bay.

# SPIDER LAKE
# RISING II

The patter of small feet descending the stairs pulled Rebecca Olson's attention away from the forty-five-inch muskie lying lifeless on the stainless steel table before her. Seated on a stool, she rolled back and waited for her girls to run in.

The seven-year-old entered first, scurrying quickly into the basement room and across its sawdust-coated floor. "Have you started yet?" she asked in breathless anticipation. The four-year-old, right at her sister's heels, eagerly asked, "Can we see what it's been eating first?" Without waiting for an answer, each girl grabbed a chair, dragged it to the table, and climbed up into a kneeling position. They were in their pajamas and ready for bed, but Rebecca had promised them a dissection before lights-out.

"You are right on time," she smiled. "I was just laying him out."

Rebecca Olson ran Wild Things Taxidermy out of her home on Jolly Fisherman Road, near Minong. She was new to the field and was slowly building a reputation and a clientele. But right now, speed was her main selling point. Since Rebecca had few clients, she had no summer backlog. This meant that she could have a fish mounted and shipped within a few weeks, rather than several months, which was the norm for taxidermists in the area. This trophy muskie, caught on Lost Land Lake, had been on ice only a few days.

"Remember to watch the knives," she cautioned and pulled closer a tray filled with shiny surgical-type instruments. The lethal tools had claws, razor-like blades, and pointy tips. Neatly laid out side by side were a skinning knife, a membrane separator, a scalpel, a hook scraper, skinning shears, and a fleshing tool. She reached for the scalpel. "Okay, let's see what this guy had for his last meal. Ready?"

The girls adjusted the headbands holding back their hair and leaned in closer. Rebecca made a long incision, just above the belly, that stretched from the muskie's gills to its tail fin. Being careful not to tear its olive skin, Rebecca opened the cut wider and wider until the animal's cold, slimy internal organs spilled out.

"Ewwwww, icky," the seven-year-old groaned, but she smiled with fascination at the mess.

"What's that?" the younger girl asked, pointing to a dark lobe barely visible among the white, gummy membranes.

"That's the liver," her mother replied.

"And that's the stomach, right?" the seven-year-old chimed in, showing off her knowledge. She reached over, touched the slimy, elongated pouch, and giggled. "It's hard. Something's in there."

"Let me feel! Let me feel!" the four-year-old squealed and shoved herself forward.

"Okay, now." Rebecca gently pushed the girls back. "Let's cut it open and see what's inside."

She took the scalpel again, pushed back the noodle-like intestines, and slowly sliced open the muskie's stomach. Using the knife, she flicked out a partially digested crawdad, searched further and found a mangled torpedo lure, and then—her girls squealing with a mixture of delight and disgust—pulled out a gooey ten-inch fish.

"What is *that*?" the older girl questioned, recoiling slightly. "It doesn't look like any fish I've ever seen."

"Me either," her sister agreed. She wrinkled up her nose. "It looks weird."

"It does," Rebecca admitted. The fish was surprisingly intact—barely digested. It really must have been this muskie's last meal. She examined the small fish, noting its markings and fin structure. "My guess is a dogfish."

The seven-year-old snickered. The four-year-old looked confused. "Does it bark?" she asked skeptically.

"No, no," her mother said, grinning. "Dogfish, or bowfin, have very large canine teeth. That's where they get the name." She carefully pulled open the animal's mouth. "See. And you can tell it's a dogfish by the very long dorsal fin." She brushed her hand along its tan, feathery fin, then abruptly stopped. She stared in puzzlement at the dogfish's belly. *That's odd*, she thought and got up from her stool. "Stay back from the table," she called over her shoulder as she walked away and to a nearby bookshelf. She ran her finger across a row of books, found the one she wanted, and pulled it out. As she flipped through the pages, Rebecca slowly walked back to the table. She sighed heavily as she placed the open book next to the fish. What the muskie had eaten was no bowfin. Bowfin had a short anal fin. This fish had a much longer one. And now that she was really looking, the markings were all wrong. This fish had the markings in the photo she was holding bookmarked by her finger. This fish was a snakehead.

"Okay, girls, enough for tonight. Time for bed," she announced hurriedly.

"Awwwww, come on, Mom," the older girl whined. "Can't we stay up longer?"

"Come on," the younger girl echoed. "Please?"

"Nope, off to bed," she ordered and whisked them up the basement stairs to where their father waited.

Rebecca had heard of the exotic snakehead fish, and she knew it was trouble. She sat back down on the stool, picked up the book, and read. The species was from Asia, and once it invaded American waters, there was no stopping it. A female could release up to seventy-five thousand eggs a year. Their fry, or young offspring, grew amazingly fast and had very good survival rates. Snakeheads were a thrust predator and would eat anything that passed, usually ingesting it whole. They were monsters that could reach lengths up to forty inches. With very few natural predators, the book said, the snakehead would become king of any lake or pond it inhabited, driving many native species to extinction.

She glanced over the top of the book at the muskie, Wisconsin's most ferocious aquatic predator, then reached out and patted the dead animal as if to say "good boy." She shook her head sadly. The small snakehead lying before her could mean the ruin of Lost Land Lake—especially if more were found in its waters.

Rebecca wrapped up the snakehead and placed it in the freezer at Wild Things Taxidermy. Tomorrow she would take the fish to the Department of Natural Resources. Tomorrow, panic would likely erupt across the county. Tomorrow, Lost Land Lake would make headlines again. *Tomorrow ...*

# BIG BLUE

Pike had the pedal to the floor of the golf cart as he, Griffy, and Spinner navigated the roller coaster that was the County A highway. Spinner leaned as far out of the vehicle as he could, trying to catch whatever breeze the converted cart could generate. Afraid the dog would fall out, Griffy kept one arm around Spinner, as he looked over the dashboard and onto the sea of bumper stickers covering the cart's army green hood. Only one stood out. It read: Escape to Wisconsin. Griffy smiled and hugged Spinner closer. His dad was coming up next week, and he really felt ready for it. Now that he had a few weeks' practice under his belt, filleting fish and running *The Lucky 13* were a breeze. Actually, everything was going smoothly at Whispering Pines Lodge, so much so that he and Pike were surprisingly bored.

"I can't believe you and I haven't done this yet," Pike said as the cart dipped down a hill.

"Well, it's kinda for little kids, right?" Griffy asked.

"Yeah, kinda. I don't think I've seen her since I was nine or ten. Still, she is soooo fat. It's hilarious."

The "she" was Big Blue, a bluegill of world record size that Sunken Island Resort kept like a pet in its small cove. Griffy couldn't believe he hadn't seen Big Blue or Sunken Island Resort, either. Both were just across the lake from Whispering Pines. *A killer muskie and that no-good archaeologist Dr. Potts might have had something to do with it*, he concluded, thinking back to the previous summers' adventures. Griffy was very glad this summer was turning out to be drama- and escapade-free. He paused and thought twice about that one. *Okay, there* had *been a little drama, but accidents really don't count.* All he wanted to do for the rest of the summer was stay accident-free, have fun, and spend time with his dad. That was it. Not too much to ask.

"There it is," Pike announced, pointing toward the woods to their right and to a small wooden sign with the words Sunken Island Resort carved across it. The sign was shaped like an arrow and directed them down a paved road. They drove past a group of vacationers playing badminton and waved to another group out on a walk before stopping in front of a neatly kept house and garage. Griffy looked around. Actually, everything was neatly kept and well organized. Not like Whispering Pines at all. Uncle Dell had stuff everywhere.

"This is a really nice place," he said as they all exited the cart. Spinner took off toward the badminton players, and Griffy soon heard someone yell out, "Hey, bring that back!" He and Pike chuckled. Spinner loved a good chase. He would steal anything—your fish, your sock, your birdie. It didn't matter.

"It is nice," Pike replied, looking around, too. "Small. They've only got four cabins." He pointed across a large grassy yard to four log buildings sitting in a row about ten feet off the shoreline. "But it's one of the cleanest resorts on Lost Land Lake." He shrugged. "At least that's what I'm told."

"I thought I heard someone pull up." The announcement interrupted the boys' conversation, and they turned to see a plump, middle-aged woman walking up. She carried gardening tools, and she tucked them under her armpit as she approached the boys with one hand extended. "Welcome. Welcome," she said, beaming, and shook hands with each of them. "I'm Betsy Wagoner."

"I'm Pike McKendrick, and this is Griffy Griffith," Pike said. Griffy cringed slightly. He wasn't used to hearing his nickname and last name together like that. It sounded strange, and he wasn't sure he liked it. Pike shot him an odd, what's-wrong-with-you look. Griffy shrugged dismissively, gave Betsy a smile, and said, "We're from Whispering Pines Lodge."

"Oh yes," she chirped happily. "I hardly recognized you. I should have recognized the cart as Dell's, though. Well, you both have grown so." She frowned. "Hair's a lot longer, too. Saw you up on that float in the muskie parade a year or so ago." She waved the palms of her hands at them. "Hold on now, and let me get Frank. We need a picture."

"Great," Pike whispered under his breath. Griffy elbowed him in the ribs.

"Frank! Frank!" Betsy called out, and soon a golf cart came roaring around the side of the house. The driver brought the vehicle to a screeching halt in front of them. As the man stood up, Griffy's eyes slowly moved skyward. The guy went up and up and up. He had to be about seven feet tall. He was super skinny with a large, protruding Adam's apple. The guy reminded Griffy of a scarecrow. He looked over at his friend with raised eyebrows.

For all his talk about Big Blue, Pike had forgotten to mention this very important detail: the owner of Sunken Island Resort was ginormous. Pike mouthed *Sorry* and nodded knowingly.

"Howdy, there. I'm Frank," the man said when he was finally standing straight.

"These two boys are those muskie catchers," Betsy said. "Let's get a couple pictures. Camera?"

"Right here," Frank said and reached into the golf cart.

"Let's get the boys over by the resort sign," Betsy directed. "Then one with you, one with me."

When all the photos were finished, Frank put an arm around Pike and Griffy's shoulders. "I bet you are here to see Big Blue. Am I right?"

"Right," Griffy nodded, looking way up and over his shoulder at the man.

"Oh boys, boys," Betsy cried softly. Her demeanor changed from bubbly to sad rather quickly. "We haven't seen Big Blue all week. I'm so worried about her. I've put all her favorite food out, but it just floats there untouched. We were really hoping to get her up to five pounds soon. I don't know now." She wrung her hands, and the sad was quickly replaced by anger. "Caught that mean little Thompson boy throwing rocks at her last week. I gave him a good talking to. You bet I did." She shook her finger sternly. "If that boy did something to Big Blue ... Well, that family won't be invited back here—ever!"

"Okay, Betsy, okay." Frank patted the air with his hand. "Calm down." He looked to the boys. "I've been meaning to check the cove out, but with my arthritis ..." He pointed way down to his knees. "The joints are a little brittle these days. Wading around and bending over just don't work. I would never ask a guest to help out, but how 'bout you two? Would you mind?"

Betsy beamed, back to bubbly again. "Oh, that would be lovely, just lovely," she nodded encouragingly.

"Sure," Pike said. He gestured toward Griffy. "We're pretty good at solving mysteries."

"Yeah," Griffy agreed. "We can check it out."

Frank bent low and climbed back into the golf cart. "Hop in. I'll drive us over."

Pike and Griffy held on tightly as the golf cart sped away and, in a few minutes, came to an abrupt halt at a small, neatly landscaped cove. *He's got to have this thing souped up big-time*, Griffy thought as he was forced to jump—or fall—out of the vehicle. Uncle Dell's cart did not go this fast. He looked around and saw a bench sitting near the water along with a sign announcing that this was the Home of Big Blue: World Record Size Bluegill.

"You know, we don't let anyone fish in the cove anymore. Not after what happened last summer," Frank explained as the boys removed their socks and shoes.

Pike's head shot up. "What happened?"

"Big Blue almost swallowed the hook. Betsy was beside herself with worry." Frank shook his head back and forth. "You know, that fish has been caught and put back in the water sixty-three times, and not once did she come close to swallowing the hook. Not until last year. I worked for hours trying to get that hook out and cause as little internal damage as possible. We thought she was a goner, but she pulled through. One close call was enough for Betsy. You can't catch Big Blue now, only feed her—if we can find her."

"No problem," Griffy said. "I'll be happy just seeing her. How big is she?"

"Four pounds, fourteen ounces. World record holder is four pounds, twelve ounces. Two ounces, and we've got our five pounds. Betsy's the one who first caught Blue. She was a fat little gal even way back then. It was Betsy's idea to screen off the cove and keep her. See how big we could get her. She's an eater. That's for sure. But she's a real hard one to catch."

The boys rolled their shorts up and got ready to explore the water. "Do you have nets, a rake, or anything?" Pike asked, looking around.

"Oh, sure," Frank answered, motioning to a wooden stand tucked into the surrounding woods. It held various garden tools and a couple of nets. "Use whatever you'd like."

Griffy took a net, Pike a rake, and then they descended into the cove's cold, dark water. It was surprisingly deep. Griffy pushed his shorts higher and made a pain-stricken face as he stepped on one sharp rock after another. As the rocks gave way to sand and the sand to slimy weeds, the look on his face changed from pain to disgust. He shuddered as sticky, gooey weeds wrapped around his ankles. He looked over at his friend. Pike didn't seem to notice or care about the weeds as he trudged toward the mouth of the cove. He seemed to have a plan, so Griffy turned and followed him.

"Just what I thought," Pike announced as he jabbed the end of the rake around.

"What? What?" Frank questioned and moved in for a better look from shore.

Pike threw the rake up on the grass, squatted down, and felt around with his hand. Griffy joined in. "Ow!" he yelled and quickly pulled his hand out of the water.

"There's a hole in the screen," Griffy explained. "I just pricked myself on it." He held up his blood-oozing finger for Frank to see.

"Yeah," Pike said. "It's down pretty low, so you can't see it from shore. I'm going to say Big Blue found an escape route and took it."

"But that's a steel mesh." Shock and puzzlement covered the adult's face. "It'd have to be cut. Who would do that? Who would want to do that?"

The boys shrugged.

"How about a muskie?" Griffy asked. "A muskie could chew through that, right?"

"No, no," Frank replied as he scratched the back of his head. "Muskies don't come in here, thanks to Sunken Island. Water's too shallow for them."

Griffy nodded. *Duh!* He knew that. Sunken Island was a large sandbar about fifteen feet from shore. It acted as a barrier. Any map of Lost Land Lake showed that pan fish and bass ruled the waters between the bar and the shore—nothing bigger.

"Maybe it was that Thompson kid," Pike offered. Griffy shot him a quit-trying-to-cause-trouble glare. A small grin surfaced on Pike's face. "Well, it could be," he replied mischievously.

Frank nodded slowly. "Yes," he agreed. "It could be." The man looked lost. He stared at the cove in a daze. "You know, Betsy has quite a rapport with Big Blue. Comes down to the cove every day and talks to her." Frank paused and looked across the well-manicured lawn. He gulped when he saw Betsy making her way toward them. "Oh, she is not going to like this," he murmured. "Brace yourselves."

About ten minutes later, the boys left Frank at the side of the cove trying to talk a hysterical Betsy out of beating the Thompson boy silly. The two snickered, as they climbed back into the cart.

"I feel sorry for that kid," Pike said.

"Really? You're the one who offered his head up on a platter," Griffy challenged.

"Hey, you saw her. She's cuckoo. I'll rat out anyone to keep Betsy off our backs."

Griffy laughed. "I'm with you. She's a little 'cuckoo for Cocoa Puffs'—that's for sure." He looked around. "Where's Spinner?"

Pike shrugged. "Dunno."

Griffy called for the dog but got no response.

Pike backed the cart up and turned it around to leave.

"Stop," Griffy ordered. "What are you doing? We can't go without Spinner."

Pike waved his friend off. "He'll find us. He always does."

And sure enough, just a few minutes later, Griffy saw Spinner bolt out of the woods and race for the cart. A tattered badminton birdie hung from his mouth.

Griffy punched Pike in the arm. "Slow down. Slow down," he ordered. "Spinner's coming."

Pike took his foot off the accelerator, waited for the dog to jump in, and then slammed his foot to the floor again.

"So, now what?" Griffy asked as the cart sped them back to the County A road. "Sunken Island was a bust."

Pike thought for a moment, then exclaimed: "Mr. Hanover! Wanna go see him? He's right up the road."

Griffy nodded, remembering the gruff old man with the thick glasses and magnified eyes. "Works for me. Let's go."

They turned right on the County A and carefully watched the side of the road for a rickety old mailbox labeled T. Hanover.

"There. See it?" Griffy pointed to a narrow opening just ahead of them.

Pike turned the cart and struggled to maneuver it down the overgrown road. "This is a lot worse than I remember," he said as he bobbed and weaved in his seat, trying to avoid the branches and brush assaulting them.

"Whoa! Slow down. Slow down," Griffy ordered and hit his friend in the arm again. "Is that a cross?" he asked. Pike followed Griffy's gaze to a small clearing in the woods. He quickly stopped the cart and jumped out, with Spinner right at his heels. "That's got to be a grave marker. Come on."

The boys cut through the woods to the grassy clearing and to the three-foot-tall cross that was made of cement and colorful lake rocks. A dog collar hung from it. Pike grabbed the collar's tag. His face immediately darkened. "It says 'Sadie.'"

Griffy lowered his head. Sadie was Mr. Hanover's German shepherd. He ran his hand over the smooth rocks. "Mr. Hanover must have made this himself," he said sadly.

Pike nodded and clapped his friend on the back. Just then, Griffy clutched his stomach and doubled over.

"Whoa. Um—um—um," Pike stammered. "You okay?" Confusion filled his voice. "It was just a dog."

Griffy looked up at Pike, shook his head slowly left to right, but didn't answer.

"Well, if it's not the dog, then what?" Pike demanded. "What's wrong? What?"

"Cramp," Griffy finally grunted. His stomach heaved violently, and then it loosened enough for him to stand up.

"Oh," was all Pike said. Then he snickered.

"What's so funny?"

"Nothing." But he kept on snickering. Griffy glared at him. "Okay, okay. I've been pooping nonstop since yesterday," Pike explained. "Whatever you've got, I've got. Must have been something we ate. Just go in the woods, so we can get going and see what's up with Mr. Hanover."

"I'm not pooping in the woods. I'm fine now." Griffy forced himself upright. "See?" Holding his side and groaning quietly, Griffy headed back to the cart, then stopped and looked around. Spinner was gone—again. He opened his mouth to call for the dog but changed his mind and continued to the cart.

Soon the boys found themselves at the end of the road and in the midst of a tan clapboard cabin, a garage, and two small outbuildings. Soft music and loud banging filled the air. Griffy had expected somber silence. He was happily surprised by the buzz of activity. As soon as Pike brought the cart to a stop, a yellow Labrador retriever pup darted from one of the outbuildings. The dog took one look at the boys, bared his teeth, and charged. Without thinking, Griffy jumped back in the cart. Pike snickered. "It's just a puppy. Scaredy-cat!"

Barking fiercely, the little dog lunged at them, jumped back, lunged again, and then jumped back. "See," Pike said. "He's more afraid of us. All bark. No bite."

"For now," Mr. Hanover called as he emerged from the same building.

Griffy stared at the old man. He had forgotten how old Mr. Hanover was. Brown age spots covered his arms, just a few wisps of white hair covered his head, and those Coke-bottle eyeglasses made his eyes look so weird.

Mr. Hanover was smirking as he came out carrying an armful of boxes. "Give her a few years," he continued. "She'll have the bite, all right." He gave a loud whistle and called. "Come, Sandy. Come." The pup looked to the boys, then to Mr. Hanover, and back to the boys again. She hesitated before finally running to her master's side. "Good girl. She's learning." He bent down and patted the dog's head. "Well now, what brings you two down my way?"

"We stopped to see Big Blue," Pike explained.

"But she's missing," Griffy finished.

"Missing?" the old man questioned sharply and stared intensely at them with his magnified eyes. "What do you mean 'missing'?" he demanded.

Griffy gulped slightly and looked at Pike, who fidgeted nervously next to the cart. Griffy hadn't seen Mr. Hanover in more than a year, and he was getting the feeling they weren't welcome here.

"A hole in the steel mesh," Griffy replied quietly. "She got out." A tense silence fell over the threesome.

Mr. Hanover let out an aggravated sigh. "Criminy. Forgive a cranky old man his bad manners. I'm glad to see you boys." He finally smiled at them. "There have been some strange goings-on around here lately. It's put me on edge."

Pike and Griffy both perked to attention. "Like what?" Pike asked.

"Yeah," Griffy piped up, relieved the old man had finally welcomed them. "We've been bored over at Whispering Pines. Nothing going on at all."

"Well, for one," Mr. Hanover pointed to the lake, "dead fish keep washing to shore. They look all chewed up, like they've been attacked. And you can't catch a tootin' thing off Sunken Island. These three young guys come every year for the crappie run. I watch 'em. They always pull in the daily limit—and then some. Been fined before. But this year they didn't catch diddly."

The boys exchanged puzzled looks. Griffy shrugged. "We haven't noticed anything by us."

"Fishing's been slow, especially in the bay, but ..." Pike's voice trailed off.

The old man dismissed it all with a quick flick of his hand; then he beckoned to them. "Come on. Don't just stand there; get on over here and help me move some of this stuff."

The boys eagerly jumped to Mr. Hanover's command. "So, what's going on here?" Griffy asked, as they approached the shed. He remembered that Mr. Hanover's garage-turned-warehouse was a dusty, disorganized mess, but the property itself was always well kept. Now, it looked like a junkyard.

"Yeah," Pike chimed in. "And what happened to Sadie?" Sympathy filled his voice. "We saw her grave."

Mr. Hanover passed some boxes to each of them. "Old age happened to Sadie," he answered matter-of-factly. "It gets us all eventually. Took her this past winter." He looked around and pointed to where the boxes should go. "I'm doing a little housecleaning, at the order of my kids, grandkids, and great-grandkids. All of 'em ganging up on me now. They don't think I can handle the place anymore." He paused. "Hmmm, they're probably right. They were right about Sandy, here. I didn't want her, not at first." Then he moved his arm in a circle. "It's all got to go."

"You're getting rid of all this stuff?" Pike asked, wide-eyed.

"Yes siree."

"Even this?" Pike quickly asked. Griffy saw the glow of excitement fill Pike's eyes, but he didn't understand why. Pike was holding what looked like a bunch of plumbing pipes. What was so exciting about that?

Mr. Hanover chuckled. "Even that. It's yours, if you take it with you today."

"What is it?" Griffy asked.

"A potato launcher," Pike answered. He looked to Mr. Hanover. "Right?"

"You betcha. Made that one for my grandson. It'll shoot an Idaho potato the length of a football field."

"Cool!" Now Griffy was excited. He moved closer to Pike and studied the launcher. It was made of white PVC pipe and stood about five feet tall, just slightly taller than he was. It reminded Griffy of a pioneer's musket, except its barrel was much wider.

"You'll need this," Mr. Hanover said as he pulled a long rod out of a junk pile.

Griffy looked puzzled. "For what?"

"Ramrod," Pike answered. "To push the potato down the barrel."

*Exactly like a musket,* Griffy thought. "Does it use gunpowder?"

"Something even better and cheaper," Mr. Hanover replied, smiling. "Hair spray."

"Hair spray?" Griffy snorted.

"Yep. Aerosol, not pump," Pike clarified. "You spray a whole bunch into the ignition chamber, here." Pike pointed to the correct spot on the launcher. "When you push the button here," he pointed again, "it sparks, ignites the fumes on fire, and BAM!— out shoots a potato." The boy smiled brightly, and his brown eyes danced in a way that made Griffy wary. He watched Pike's smile quickly turn into a mischievous grin. "Can we try it—now?"

Mr. Hanover's face furrowed with thought. "Don't think I have any hair spray around here." He rubbed his chin as he glanced here and there. "Where? Where would it be?" he chanted and shook his finger at the two boys, as if the movement would help him to remember. But just then, an alarmed bark filled the air and turned the attention of all three to Lost Land Lake. The bark rang out again.

"That sounds like Spinner," Pike said.

"Yeah," Griffy agreed. "He's not happy about something."

Sandy, who was sniffing around a pile of old work boots, cocked her head to one side and listened, too. Suddenly, she started barking and bolted toward the lake. Griffy and Pike exchanged perplexed looks as the dog raced by them. Without saying a word, they turned together and sprinted after Sandy.

"Whoa, there. Whoa!" Mr. Hanover called after the dog. "Stay! Sandy! Stay!" But the pup was long gone. "Oh, criminy," the old man huffed and ran after the group.

The boys found Spinner at the water's edge, yapping and pawing at a pile of weeds and muck that had washed ashore. Sandy darted up to the scene, barked crazily at Spinner, and then darted away. Spinner looked up as the boys approached. He raised his white bushy eyebrows and summoned them with a bark and a paw to the weed pile.

"He wants us to take a look," Griffy said.

The boys pushed the dog back and began digging through the slimy weeds. Griffy suddenly recoiled and jumped up. "Yuck!" The hollow eye socket of a dead fish stared at him from out of the muck. He grimaced and wiped his hands on his shorts and T-shirt.

Pike dug faster, pulling weeds off the dead fish and throwing them haphazardly over his shoulder. "Oh no," he cried out. He stopped digging, too and sat with shoulders slumped, looking down at the weeds.

"What?" Griffy questioned.

Mr. Hanover finally trotted up to Griffy's side. "Yes, boy, spit it out. What?" Panting heavily, he looked down and murmured, "Oh no."

Griffy looked from one to the other in puzzlement.

"It's Big Blue," Pike finally said, and he pulled the dead fish out of the weeds. "Her eyes are gone, and her tail is missing, but otherwise she's fat and intact. There's no mistaking it. It's Big Blue."

Mr. Hanover took the fish from Pike and examined the carcass. "The tail's not just missing, son. It's been torn right off poor Blue's body. Look at the shredded flesh."

Griffy gulped. "What would have done that? It wouldn't be a muskie, right? Not here by Sunken Island."

The old man shrugged. "Well, anything is possible, I suppose. But it's not likely. This water is too shallow for muskies, and Big Blue wouldn't swim too far from home, not after all these years of being fed in captivity. Besides, a muskie wouldn't attack and leave a fish injured like this. A muskie would have eaten Big Blue." Mr. Hanover looked out across Lost Land Lake. "Strange goings-on, I say. Strange."

His tone sent a shiver down Griffy's spine. He and Pike stared nervously at the dead fish in the old man's hands.

Pike looked over at his friend. "Betsy is *really* not gonna like this."

Griffy suddenly felt very sorry for that Thompson boy. As if on cue, his stomach let out a long, low groan and rumbled vigorously. He held it tightly and gritted his teeth. *Strange things are going on, all right,* he thought just as he doubled over in pain.

# Spider Lake
# Rising III

About the time Griffy and Pike were heading down the road to Mr. Hanover's, the panic that Rebecca Olson at Wild Things Taxidermy had predicted began to spread. When she walked out of Minong's Department of Natural Resources headquarters, Rebecca left behind a ten-inch snakehead fish and a whirlwind of activity. As she passed Village Hall, just blocks down the street, the phone in Andy Gibson's office was already ringing. He ran in and reached over his desk to answer it. "Chequamegon Lake Association. President Gibson here." His face clouded, and then all expression left it. Andy listened intently to the caller as he twirled a piece of straw back and forth in his mouth. His jaw suddenly dropped open, and the straw fell to the ground.

Fifteen miles away, on Spider Lake, DNR ranger Matt Mullen's VHF radio squawked to life as he steered his boat toward the dock at Empire Lodge. He cut the motor and picked up the receiver. "Mullen. Go ahead." As he listened, his eyes slowly glassed over. He mouthed the words *Holy cow* just as the boat bumped up against the wooden dock. "Dang it," he huffed out loud and quickly grabbed the boat's steering wheel. The radio receiver slipped from his hand. "Dang it," he repeated. Matt reached for the dock's edge with one hand and fumbled for the receiver cord with the other. Holding the boat steady against the dock, he yanked the cord, flipped the receiver into the air, caught it with one hand, and pushed the Talk button. "Roger that. Will do," he said flatly, as if nothing had happened. "ETA is two hours. Just wrapping up Spider Lake patrol. Over."

Matt was being called back to DNR headquarters. A northern snakehead had been found in the stomach of a muskie caught on Lost Land Lake. He shook his head angrily. *Not good.* Part of the reason he had become a DNR ranger was to protect and preserve the lakes he'd grown up on, the lakes of the Chequamegon National Forest. This type of carelessness and ignorance really set him off. *So stupid!* He tied his boat to the dock and looked along the shoreline. *Know your enemy,* he thought and flashed a cunning grin. He knew the snakehead very well. It was on the US Fish and Wildlife Service's list of most injurious species, and it was illegal to import or own one. *People just don't get it,* his mind ranted. He was angry that people never thought about the consequences of their actions. That type of fish could cause irreparable damage to the ecosystem of a lake. Forget the obvious fact that invasive species competed with native animals for food and habitat. They also carried parasites and diseases. They could breed with native fish and create genetic problems. That type of fish could ruin a lake and the livelihood of every person on it. His eyes glassed over again, as his mind ranted on. *People buy these aggressive exotic fish for pets and then can't handle them. But do they kill the fish? No, that would be too cruel. Do they call the DNR? No, that would mean a fine. They do the most stupid thing: they release the fish into local waters!*

His eyes slowly cleared and refocused on the water off the shore of Empire Lodge. His simmering anger started to bubble. *Speaking of stupid, did she really think I wouldn't notice this?* His glare moved across the water, across the patchy grounds, and up to the resort's green-stained plank cabins.

Matt had been watching the area since last summer. A thick weed bed covered this part of Spider Lake, from about twenty feet out all the way to the shore, but the weeds along the shore near the resort were getting suspiciously thinner. *She's slowly clearing her swim area. No doubt about it.* The clearing of weeds was a big problem on resort lakes. Vacationers didn't like to swim or wade where slimy, sticky weeds could slither around them. But altering the lake or shoreline in any way was strictly prohibited by the DNR and the Chequamegon Lake Association. Matt had been hoping he wouldn't have to issue a warning or start the official documentation process, but it looked as if he would have to now. *She, of all people, knows better,* he silently scolded. Matt put on a pair of waders, grabbed a camera and tape measure, and then vaulted his stocky frame over the boat's edge and into Spider Lake.

Thirty minutes later, the owner of Empire Lodge stood on the dock watching Matt Mullen's boat cut across the waters of Spider

Lake. She heard the motor rev louder, and she stared as if in a trance at the foaming wake the speeding boat left behind it. She continued staring, arms locked across her chest, long after the boat had sped around the bend and out of sight. Mullen had issued her a warning about the weeds. She'd known he'd been watching. *But what was she supposed to do?* Bills were piling up. Foreclosure was looming. The other resorts on Spider Lake had nice, clear, sandy shorelines. Sunbathing and swimming were big parts of a resort's draw. No one wanted to swim in a weed bed. She knew he'd noticed the thinning weeds last summer, but she had hoped he'd ignore it. *Just let it go—but no, not Matt Mullen.* He was a by-the-book kind of guy. And it was just her luck that Matt Mullen patrolled Spider Lake. Other rangers would have looked the other way—she knew that for a fact—but not him. She let out a sour grunt. Luck never seemed to be on her side, not even when it came to a well-thought-out sabotage plan.

Mullen had told her about the emergency call back to DNR headquarters that afternoon. She now knew one of the snakeheads had been found. Word of that discovery would spread fast, which was good, but not what she really wanted, not just yet. She needed those snakeheads to stay in Lost Land Lake, mature, and spawn next year. Once those snakeheads started laying eggs by the thousands, there would be no hope for Lost Land Lake. But what if the snakeheads didn't survive? With one gone so quickly, the odds weren't good.

*That Dr. Potts,* she growled inwardly. *What a louse!* Her upper lip curled at the thought of the discredited, dishonorable archaeologist. Again, luck had not been on her side. Potts had had no problem stealing ancient fossils, but when it came to importing illegal fish—well, that was just going too far for him. *I asked for grown snakeheads, not young fry!* she fumed. But Potts had refused, insisting the grown fish were too easily tracked and traced. Too risky, he'd said. *We'll just see about that.* She knew Potts had gotten the snakehead offspring from some people in Chicago's Chinatown. In their native land, snakeheads were considered a delicacy. The fish were thought to have healing powers and were used in soups for the sick. It had been easy enough for her to find a live-fish market sympathetic to the needs of an ill grandmother and willing to ship two full-grown snakeheads to Wisconsin. *Sympathetic to my long-dead grandmother, that is You want a job done right, don't ask a man to do it.*

She thought for a moment and then grinned shrewdly. *I wonder if the* Minong Ledger *knows about this afternoon's DNR meeting?* With that, she turned and walked down the dock, back toward Empire Lodge. She had a few calls to make.

# LOCKED AND
# LOADED

Griffy and Pike wanted nothing to do with telling Betsy about Big Blue's demise. They used Griffy's rumbling stomach as an excuse and left Mr. Hanover to deal with that one. About half an hour later, Griffy's stomach cramps had passed, and the boys were back at Whispering Pines. As soon as Pike parked the cart in the garage, he jumped out. Griffy thought his friend was going to run for the lodge and get Uncle Dell. He was about to stop him and tell him that he felt fine now, but then he saw the sparkle in Pike's eyes and realized his friend's behavior had absolutely nothing to do with him. Pike grabbed the potato launcher from the back of the cart. *Of course—how silly of me*, Griffy thought. Pike had a one-track mind, and the potato launcher was on it, nothing else.

"Come on," he cried, looking impatiently at Griffy, who was

still seated in the front seat. "What are you waiting for? Let's try this thing out."

"We need hair spray, remember?" Griffy replied. "We don't have any."

"Oh, yes we do," Pike chirped happily. He practically skipped over to a column of shelves, reached up, and pulled down a large box. As he struggled with its weight and size, it hit him on the head and wobbled there precariously. "Sweet Brie! Get off your rear and help me here," he ordered.

Griffy chuckled and quickly moved to help Pike. He pushed the box off his friend's head, and together they slowly lowered it to the garage floor.

"Dell puts everything guests leave behind in here," Pike explained as he rummaged through the box. "I know we've got hair spray. Just know it."

He handed Griffy one item after another, until he finally yelled out, "Got it!" and pulled a large can of aerosol hair spray from the box.

"I'll get the potatoes," Griffy announced excitedly and took off running for the lodge. "Meet you at Suicide Rock," he called over his shoulder. Less than a minute later, he reached the landmark boulder, panting for breath and carrying four medium-sized brown potatoes.

They wasted no time loading the launcher. Pike filled the ignition chamber with hair spray. He aimed the barrel toward the middle of Lost Land Lake and, without hesitating, pushed the ignition button. The gun fired immediately, with a loud bang and burst of flames. The potato sailed through the air and landed with a *plop* in the lake. The boys exchanged shocked, excited looks. Their eyes lit up.

"Holy chedda cheese!" Pike exclaimed. "Did you see the distance that got?"

Griffy nodded enthusiastically. "And the flame. Did you see it? It's a potato launcher and flamethrower all in one." Griffy thought for a moment. "Hey, go over to the swim bay." He pointed across the peninsula. "Let's see if we can control it. You know, hit a target."

Pike didn't need to be told twice. He took off in a sprint and waved his hands high overhead when he was in place and ready. "How's this?" he yelled.

Griffy gave him a thumbs-up. He loaded the potato, aimed the gun, and fired. The potato overshot Pike, but just by a few feet. *Not bad*, he thought. He looked the launcher up and down. It would have to be big, but with a little practice, this thing could hit a target, no problem.

"Good shot!" Pike yelled and ran back to Griffy. "My turn. You've got to see it from that end." He burst into a silly giggle. "The potato looks like a flying piece of poop. It's crazy."

Griffy ran across the peninsula and got into position as Pike fired. He watched the disfigured potato soar up into the blue sky. *It does look like a piece of poop!* He snickered as the potato flew closer and closer—and then went over his head. Shielding his eyes with his hand, he turned to follow its path, but he lost it in the sun. He listened for the splash, but one never came. Instead, a series of high-pitched shrieks filled the swim bay. *Girls!* When he turned back, Pike had run up beside him. He said to Pike, "You overshot—by a lot. I think you hit the swim raft!"

"Nope, didn't overshoot," Pike grinned slyly. "I hit my intended target." He brushed the palms of his hands together and chuckled. "Gil and the Garfield sisters are sunbathing on that raft."

"Ohhhhhh," Griffy groaned and looked apprehensively toward the swim bay. "You are going to be in *so* much trouble. They'll kill you."

"Not if they don't know it's us." Pike pointed to the lush woods surrounding the swim bay.

"Us?" Griffy questioned. "Oh no!"

"Come on, wimp." Pike raised his eyebrows up and down and motioned enticingly toward the woods.

Griffy laughed and quickly returned Pike's mischievous look. "Okay, but we need more ammo," he said and directed his friend toward the lodge. The two took off in a full-out sprint.

About five minutes later, the boys were in position, crouched behind a cluster of four white birch trees. The swim raft sat straight ahead, about thirty feet from shore. Griffy scratched his face and batted away the tall grass and ferns surrounding them. A sack of brown potatoes rested on a patch of moss at his knees. *Moss makes a great cushion*, he thought as his knees sunk into the thick, moist greenery. Pike quickly laid out their plan of attack.

"I'm thinking we don't want to *actually* hit the raft," he was saying as he peered through the tree branches. "But aim for the water a few feet off it." He pointed left and right. "Soak 'em, not slay 'em. What do you think?"

Griffy thought that was an unusually wise plan for Pike. If one of those girls took a potato to the head, he and Pike wouldn't see blue sky or daylight for the rest of the summer. Griffy slapped a potato into his friend's hand. "Lock and load it," he ordered.

Pike grinned ear to ear as he loaded the launcher. Griffy grabbed the ramrod and forced the vegetable down the long barrel. Pike aimed the gun high, and within seconds he fired the first shot. *Whooooommmp!* The potato blasted out of the barrel, dropped from the sky, and plunged into the shimmering water. The lake erupted like a geyser and soaked the left side of the swim raft. Jill Garfield screamed as cold water hit her. All three teenagers jumped up. *Perfect shot!* Pike loaded and fired off another round and then another. A broad grin spread across Griffy's face as the raft broke out in chaos, with bikini-clad girls squealing and scrambling across the platform. "My turn. My turn," he pleaded impatiently and reached for the launcher. Pike reluctantly gave it up.

As Pike loaded in a potato, Griffy sprayed hair spray into the ignition chamber. He took aim, pointing the barrel through the fluttering birch leaves, and fired. *Whoooosh!* The potato left the launcher in a burst of flames. *Splat!* It hit the side of the raft and spewed potato chunks all over Pike's sister. She shrieked and stomped her feet, as the Garfield sisters picked potato out of her long, dark-brown hair. Griffy cringed. *Oops.*

Just then Griffy felt a strong hand clamp down on his shoulder. He glanced at Pike, who was standing right beside him, and saw a large hand clamped on him, too. Griffy slowly moved only his head and eyes to look over his shoulder and up into the scowling face of Uncle Dell.

"I think you two are done here," his uncle announced sternly. He glared down at Griffy and ordered, "Drop it." Griffy's grip on the gun loosened immediately, and it slowly fell onto the mossy ground. "Why don't you boys go over to the *other* bay and do some fishing. We could use some for dinner this week. Guests can't seem to catch any bluegill around here. Doing a lot of complaining about it. Why don't you show 'em how it's done."

Uncle Dell didn't wait for an answer; instead, he turned the boys around and escorted them out of the woods. As they reluctantly marched away, Griffy and Pike turned their heads and looked with sad longing back to where the potato launcher had fallen.

Across the peninsula, an hour later, Griffy reeled in what seemed to be his one hundredth cast into Whispering Pines Bay. Neither he nor Pike had had a bite. *Very strange*, Griffy thought. Bluegill, pumpkinseed, rock bass, and even perch schooled in this bay. He remembered the conversation they had had with Mr. Hanover and chuckled. The elderly man had been right. They couldn't catch a tootin' thing. Griffy eyed the brown night crawler impaled on his hook. It was the same one he had started with. The worm was still intact but looking a little soggy now. *Might need one with a little more wiggle*, he thought.

"This stinks," Pike grumbled as he cast out again. "What do you think Dell will do with the potato launcher? Do you think we'll get it back? Huh? Do you?"

Griffy shrugged. "He won't throw it away or anything, but we might not ever see it again."

Pike's face dropped into a pout. "That's what I was afraid—"

"Holy chedda cheese!" Griffy yelled, cutting Pike off midsentence. His fishing pole dipped sharply downward. He jerked the pole upward and instantly felt a strong pull back. "I got one! A big one!" His face twisted into a mixture of determination and eager anticipation, as he struggled to bring the fish in. When the animal's head finally broke the water's surface, he and Pike exchanged dumbfounded looks. Its head was flat, like a snake's. Griffy's eyes narrowed. It couldn't be. Lost Land Lake didn't have water snakes. He reeled faster, jettisoning the animal through the water toward him. When he pulled the fish onto the sandy shore, both boys stared down at the skinny eel-like creature, until Pike finally heaved out a frustrated sigh.

"You gotta be kidding me. That's a dogfish." He flipped the fish over with his foot. "Yep, I haven't seen one in years." He shook his head in disgust. "We've been out here for hours, and this is what we catch. A stinkin' dogfish."

"Well, it was fun. The thing put up a really good fight. Look at it. It's not even a foot long and real skinny."

Pike shrugged dismissively. He seemed more repulsed by this fish than by the puffy-mouthed suckers they caught at the dam. Griffy didn't understand how that could be. The dogfish looked scary with its pointy head and long feathery fins, but it wasn't that bad. He looked curiously at the fish. "What's so wrong with it? Besides being ugly."

"It's a trash fish," Pike explained. "No one wants 'em. Not good to eat and not a game fish like the muskie." His face twisted into a sour scowl as he spoke. "They are predators and fierce. Strong jaws. Sharp teeth. They'll rip apart your best lure, for sure."

"Okay, got it." Griffy nodded and picked up the dogfish. Gripping it tightly, he removed the hook from its mouth. "Back in the water for you, then."

"No!" Pike shouted and quickly grabbed his friend's arm. "You're not getting it. We don't want dogfish in Lost Land Lake. They eat the good fish. They destroy your lures. They—"

"Pike!"

He stopped abruptly, and his head spun around in the direction of the annoyed shout. Griffy followed Pike's look across the peninsula. *Gil.*

"Uh-oh. She's not happy," Pike whispered.

"It's time to go. Now!" his sister ordered.

"Coming!" he called and turned back to Griffy. "Get rid of it," he instructed and jogged up the embankment a few steps. Jogging in place, he turned back again. "Bury it. Do whatever. Just don't put it back in the lake." With that, he turned away and ran toward Gil.

*Bury it,* Griffy thought as he watched Pike go. *Great.* He looked at the strange olive-colored fish he held with one finger stuck under its gills, and then out to the lake. He shrugged helplessly. *Fine. I'll bury the creepy thing.* Fish in hand, he headed up the embankment himself and toward the woods on the far side of the lodge. On the way, he stopped to look for a shovel in the freezer house. Uncle Dell kept supplies in most of the outbuildings. When Griffy flipped the latch on the brown clapboard door and stepped inside, the hum of machinery instantly filled the air. A large chest freezer lined the wall to his left. On his right he passed a metal counter equipped with a roll of shiny white butcher paper and a deep porcelain sink. He dropped the dogfish in the sink and kept moving toward the back of the building, where an array of tools and other items were stacked. Griffy sorted through the supplies until he found a small shovel. *Perfect.* As he reached for it, his lower body heaved and released a low guttural rumble. He froze. *Oh no.* Looks of dread and panic came over his face. His bowels roared. Griffy doubled over and stumbled into the rakes, hoes, and shovels. They crashed to the floor around him. As he bounced up and down, trying to keep his bowels from exploding, his eyes locked on a rusty old bucket. He could drop his shorts right then and there. Pike would do it, for sure. Who would know? *Uncle Dell,* he answered himself. And Dell would make Griffy clean it up. Still bent over and staring down at the bucket,

Griffy took a deep breath, bit down hard on his lip, and squeezed his buttocks together even harder. He turned quickly and, like a crazed speed walker, hustled himself out of the freezer house. The sound of slamming doors followed him in steady succession: Freezer house—BANG! Lodge—BANG! Bathroom—BANG!

Griffy dropped his shorts, sat, and sighed with relief: *Whew! Made it.*

# POOP, PARASITES, AND PREDATORS

The next morning, Griffy was up and in the bathroom early. He needed to poop but instead stood staring into the toilet at the white plastic cone sitting in the bowl. In one hand, he held a small clear vial, in the other a wooden tongue depressor. He yawned, stuck the depressor in his matted brown hair, and scratched his head with it. Then, he turned around, dropped his pajama pants and sat down.

After Griffy's frantic race to the toilet the evening before, Uncle Dell insisted on taking him to the hospital. Griffy wanted nothing to do with that. The two had argued about it all through dinner. Griffy kept insisting he was fine and did not need a doctor. His dad was coming to Whispering Pines that very weekend, and the last thing Griffy wanted was for his dad to think he was sick. That would ruin all his plans. He wasn't sick, and he wasn't going to be sick. Whatever he had would pass without the help of a doctor. But Uncle Dell wouldn't listen, and he called Pike's parents, to find out that Pike had been in the bathroom since before dinner. That was all it took. They all met at the Minong Clinic an hour later. Pike and Griffy's symptoms turned out to be exactly the same: no fever, no chills, no headaches, no vomiting, just violent stomach cramps followed by lots and lots of pooping. To find the cause, the clinic doctor needed three days' worth of stool samples. That's where the cone came in.

When Griffy finished his business on the toilet, he stood up and reluctantly turned around. He eyed the cone's contents. *This is so gross.* Griffy took a deep breath and slowly blew out the air. *A guy's got to do what a guy's got to do.* He took the tongue depressor and started scooping.

As Griffy sat his first filled vial on the bathroom counter, he heard the phone ring. It was a little early for phone calls, he thought. He went into the kitchen, where his uncle was at the stove making breakfast. Dell had put the phone on speaker and was dropping bacon into a frying pan as he answered the call. "Hello. This is Whispering Pines Lodge. Dell Evers speaking."

"Dell. Good morning. Andy here. Sorry to call so early."

Griffy knew the caller was Andy Gibson, president of the Chequamegon Lake Association. Something must be up, he thought as he took a seat at the kitchen table. Andy rarely called. He liked to conduct business and share his publicity ideas for Lost Land Lake in person, usually over coffee at Spider Lake Cafe.

"Got some bad news to report. I'm calling all the businesses and resorts on Lost Land Lake. Just hung up with The Happy Hooker. We've got trouble."

Uncle Dell turned off the stove, moved the skillet to a back burner, and gave the phone his full attention. "All right, out with it, then," he said.

Griffy inched his chair closer and leaned in. He and Uncle Dell exchanged worried looks, as Andy described the snakehead fish found in Lost Land Lake. Griffy gulped. *That's got to be what got Big Blue*, he thought.

"We wanted to keep it quiet," Andy was explaining. "At least until we knew exactly how serious the situation was and what steps to take, but the *Ledger* got a hold of the story. Someone must have leaked it. I've been on the phone all night with the publisher, pleading with her not to run the story now, to just wait a few days." He paused and sighed wearily. "It's in this morning's paper. Front page."

Uncle Dell pointed to Griffy, then pointed and nodded his head toward the lodge's lobby. Griffy jumped up and raced to retrieve the newspaper. When he returned to the kitchen, Andy was gone, off breaking the news to someone else, Griffy guessed. Uncle Dell took the paper from him, quickly pulled off the rubber band surrounding it, and laid it out on the table for both to see. There it was, top story on the front page. Griffy read the headline: "Deadly Fish Found in Lost Land Lake. Local Taxidermist Discovers Snakehead in Belly of Mount." He looked up at his uncle and saw the wrinkles and crevices on Dell's face sink deeper. Uncle Dell continued reading as he picked the newspaper up, gave it a firm shake, and folded the front page over. Griffy saw a flier fall out of the pages, slowly drift to the floor, and come to a rest under the table. Curious, he bent over and cocked his head downward for a better look. WANTED: DEAD, NOT ALIVE the flier announced in full capital letters. It was some sort of wanted poster with a picture of … Griffy quickly got down on all fours and grabbed the flier. He sat under the table, studied the picture, and read: Northern Snakehead. If you come across this fish, DO NOT RELEASE. Please KILL this fish by cutting off the head or freezing, and report all catches to your local Department of Natural Resources.

The flier had a picture of the northern snakehead and listed its distinguishing features: long dorsal fin, small flat head, large mouth, big teeth, lengths up to forty inches, weight up to fifteen pounds.

*It couldn't be.*

He pulled the flier closer to his face and stared long and hard at it. *No, he had to be wrong, just had to be.* Griffy crawled from under the table toward Dell and tugged on the leg of his plaid pajamas. His uncle pulled the newspaper to one side and looked down quizzically. Griffy handed him the "Wanted" poster. "What's this?" Dell asked.

Griffy crawled farther out and stood up. He tapped the snakehead picture with his finger. "I think I caught one of these yesterday—in Whispering Pines Bay. Pike said it was a dogfish, but its hea—"

Uncle Dell abruptly cut him off. "What did you do with it? Did you release it?"

Griffy shook his head. "Nuh-uh. Pike said to bury it."

"Good. Good." His uncle smiled.

"But I didn't." The smile disappeared. "I was going to," Griffy hurriedly continued. "But then I had to go to the bathroom real, real bad."

"Well then, what happened to it?" his uncle demanded.

"I don't know," Griffy whined. "I don't remember."

"Well, think—think! Where did you go? What did you do? We

70

need to find that fish. The article here says these Asian snakeheads look very similar to dogfish." He rattled the newspaper at Griffy. "Folks can mistake the two—easily."

Griffy thought back to the afternoon before. He remembered catching the dogfish, and then his mad rush to the bathroom, but that was about it. *Where had he gone? Where? Where?* "The freezer house!" he shouted. "I went to the freezer house for a shovel." His face furrowed deeper in thought. *But what did I do with that ugly fish?*

"Come on boy, think," his uncle prodded. Griffy felt Dell's firm grip on his shoulder, and the answered suddenly popped into his head. "The sink! I dropped it in the freezer house sink."

"Good move." Uncle Dell nodded his approval. "Let's go see."

Still in their pajamas, the two made their way to the freezer house through the thick, misty morning air. The bottoms of Griffy's pajama pants quickly became caked with damp sand, dirt, and pine needles as they walked across the dew-covered ground. Shivering more from a case of the creeps than from the cool air, Griffy unlatched the freezer house door and stepped into the dark, humming room. Dell flicked the light switch on as Griffy headed straight for the sink. The dripping faucet added to the creepiness of the morning, and Griffy hesitated before peering into the deep basin. "It's still here," he called over his shoulder. Griffy sort of felt sorry for the animal. Being left out of water all night, it must have suffered as it died. Uncle Dell walked up behind him and reached down for the fish. The animal suddenly flipped, lunged forward, and sunk its mouthful of sharp teeth into Dell's hand.

"Son of gun!" he yelled and slammed his hand into the side of the sink. The blow knocked the fish out cold.

"Whoooooaaa!" was all Griffy could manage to squeak out.

As Uncle Dell loosened the animal's bite on his hand, Griffy found his voice and stammered. "How, how …?" He stopped and grunted to clear the nerves from his throat. "It's still alive," he finally got out. "How can it still be alive?"

"Don't know," his uncle answered as the fish fell from his hand and landed with a small splat back in the sink. Both stared down at the strange fish.

"But that's not a dogfish," Uncle Dell announced. "That's got to be one of those snakeheads." He paused. "Two found now." Griffy watched a look of despair fill his uncle's face. "Two," he repeated. "We better go call the DNR."

$$* \quad * \quad * \quad *$$

An hour later, a small crowd milled nervously about the lobby of Whispering Pines Lodge, drinking coffee and softly talking together. Griffy's chest felt heavier and heavier as he looked around the tension-filled room. Andy Gibson leaned against the edge of a table, twirling a piece of straw in his mouth as he listened to Pike's dad, Mitch McKendrick, talking. Pike and Gil stood with Danny Rubedieux, the blind young man and former pro hockey player who owned Sleepy Eye Rentals. One of Danny's assistants poured coffee into mugs nearby, as Jo Patterson, the DNR ranger covering Lost Land Lake, sipped the steaming beverage with Uncle Dell and a few Whispering Pines guests over by the bumper-pool table. They were all waiting for DNR ranger Matt Mullen to arrive. Griffy had learned that Mullen was the resident expert on invasive species, specifically the northern snakehead. When the bell on the lobby door announced Mullen's arrival, the crowd moved like sheep toward him.

Mullen's eyes scanned the room. "Where is it?" he asked sharply.

Uncle Dell stepped forward and waved him over to a large cooler filled with ice. "It's in there. It's still alive, barely, but still alive after a night out of water."

"Yep," Mullen nodded. "They can survive three days out of water. All they need is moisture."

The crowd murmured its surprise and moved with Mullen to the cooler. Griffy and Pike pushed to the front until each boy flanked Mullen's stocky frame. The ranger barely reacted when he opened the cooler, just muttered something under his breath. Griffy thought he made out the words *crazy* and *stupid*. Mullen picked the snakehead out of the ice, closed the cooler lid, and laid the fish neatly on top. A blur of shiny metal suddenly cut through the air. Griffy and Pike jumped back as the blade of a small machete landed on the cooler with a dull thud. The animal's flat, snakelike head tumbled to the floor.

Griffy's jaw fell open. He heard Gil shriek somewhere behind him and heard Pike gasp, "Holy chedda cheese." Pike then let out a bemused snort. "Cool." Both boys looked up at Mullen, Pike with wide-eyed admiration and Griffy with wide-eyed shock.

"Dead now," the ranger announced and re-holstered the machete in a sheath on his massive belt. He turned to the crowd. "Well, we've got ourselves a situation here. Good news is these snakeheads aren't old enough to reproduce—yet. Bad news is with two found, we're going to have to take steps."

The crowd murmured softly. Conversation erupted among the onlookers.

"Steps?" Pike's dad raised his voice above the rumble. "What do you mean by 'steps'?"

Everyone quieted down again.

"Electro-fishing will be the first. See if we find any more."

Mitch nodded, and the crowd murmured again.

Danny Rubedieux spoke up next. "What's the deal with this electro-fishing?" Gil, who was standing next to him, added: "Will it harm the lake, the other fish?"

DNR ranger Jo Patterson stepped forward. "No, not at all. It is the least harmful way to take a lake survey. A small electric current stuns the fish. They'll simply float to the surface. Within a few minutes, the stun wears off, and a large percentage of the wildlife will be just fine."

Mullen gave a nod. "That's right. We'll likely do a large-scale shocking and netting operation. Lake access will be restricted for several days."

"Restricted in what way?" Uncle Dell asked.

"No access."

The disapproving crowd flared up. Griffy and Pike exchanged shocked looks, as Andy Gibson's voice rose above the rest. "You can't close the lake for days. That will jeopardize every business on it. I won't allow it. I won't authorize it."

Stoic among the uprising, Mullen held up his hand to ask for silence. The crowd slowly quieted down.

"There's no choice. It has to be done. If there are more snakeheads, you could have yourself a full-blown invasion. They could have already spawned. If that's the case, it's over. Might as well rename the lake Lake Frankenfish."

"Lake Frankenfish?" Pike snickered.

Mullen turned his head toward the boy and grinned slightly. "One of their many nicknames." Pike returned the grin and nodded his understanding.

"All right, now." Andy took the ever-present piece of straw out of his mouth and pointed it at Mullen. "What exactly do you mean by 'over'?" he demanded.

"These fish can adapt to any environment," Mullen lectured. "They can survive both warm and cold conditions. And they lay thousands of eggs. They'll overtake the lake population in no time. But it's not just the eggs you have to worry about. This species is from Asia and carries with it parasites and diseases foreign to our waters."

"So there's no way to control them?" Danny asked. "Like draining the lake? Something?"

Mullen shook his head. "The lake's too large to drain."

"There is another option," Jo announced. She tucked her dark-blonde hair behind an ear and stepped uneasily in front of Mullen. His face clouded. "Lost Land Lake could be poisoned," she said.

"Poisoned!" Griffy blurted out. "But that would kill everything, wouldn't it?"

"Yes, it would. The lake would have to be restocked." The crowd rumbled angrily. Jo looked around the room. "We all need to realize that an entire lake system is in jeopardy. Lost Land Lake connects to Big Crooked Lake, which connects to Clam Lake. It—"

Jo abruptly stopped talking, as Mullen squeezed her arm, hard. Her hand flew to a bandage covering her forearm. Griffy wondered how Jo had hurt herself as he watched Mullen move to the front again and take charge of the crowd. "Let's all calm down." The ranger patted the air with his hands as he spoke. "There's no need to discuss drastic measures until we know where we stand. We all good with that?"

The crowd sluggishly murmured its agreement, but Mitch had

one more question. "You mentioned parasites." He looked at Pike and Griffy. "Would there be any that harm people?"

"Oh, sure. Snakeheads can carry intestinal flukes, liver flukes, that sort of thing."

Griffy raised his eyebrows and looked reproachfully at his uncle. "What's a fluke?" he asked. He could hear Gil snicker somewhere behind him.

Uncle Dell grinned meekly before answering. "It's a parasite, a flatworm."

"Another flatworm," Griffy bellowed. "You're kidding me, right? Like duck itch?"

Uncle Dell hemmed and hawed. "Sort of. You're a good host for this type, though. If you've got one, it likely won't die on its own."

"Oh, that's just *grrrreat*!" Griffy rubbed his hands across his face miserably.

Last summer, a flatworm parasite had turned his body into one big, itchy red welt, and now it looked as if another one had turned his body into one big pooping machine. Griffy slouched in defeat. Why did this have to happen now? Why couldn't it wait a couple of weeks? His dad would be here in just a few days. *Why? Why? Why?* he wondered.

Pike walked over to his friend and put his arm on his shoulder. "So, we've got worms. No big deal." He started to smile, but then his face contorted in anguish, and he stared in a frozen panic at Griffy.

Griffy knew the look well. "Bathroom. This way. Quick," he instructed and ushered Pike through the lobby. "No big deal," he teased. "Got the cone all ready for you."

# IT'S ALL BAD

Griffy sat on the bank of Whispering Pines Bay, staring out at Lost Land Lake. His elbows rested on his knees and his chin on his palms as he watched two DNR boats slowly trolling the waters. Today was the last day of electro-fishing, and the boats out on the lake were heavily equipped with nets, generators, probes, and current pulsators. So far, only one more snakehead fish had been found. That fish, like the others, had been too young to spawn, and the DNR had not located any egg nests. That was good news, but that was the only good news Griffy had heard this week.

Spinner lay at the boy's feet, chin on his paws, looking up with pitiful eyes into Griffy's drooping face. The boy glanced downward and sighed. "I know. I know," he confessed to the dog. "But I can't help it." Spinner raised his bushy eyebrows slightly, and his eyes turned into big, sad saucers. "Hey, don't look at me like that. You know everything that's happened. You know everything went bad."

The bad had started with the boys' stool test results. *Surprise, surprise,* Griffy thought sarcastically. He and Pike both had at least one Asian fluke living in their intestines. That didn't go over well—with anyone. Somehow word had gotten to the *Ledger,* and the paper immediately linked the boys' conditions to Lost Land Lake's snakehead invasion. "Boys Infected with Asian Parasite. Snakeheads Contaminate Lost Land Lake," the front-page headline had read. Griffy huffed. Obviously, nothing else newsworthy had been happening that day, or any day that week. The *Ledger* had published a front-page article every day about Lost Land Lake's vicious, monstrous snakehead fish. So, of course, his dad had found out.

Griffy stared more intently at the lake. The water sparkled as the sun danced across it, creating a hypnotic effect on the boy. He felt himself falling under its spell as the water blurred out of focus, and memories drifted through his mind. The phone call had lasted all of five minutes: "Now is just not a good time, son. You're sick; the lake's closed. I'd just be in the way."

"I'm not that sick, Dad. Really," Griffy had pleaded.

"This is best, Corbett."

"The doctor said Pike and I will be fine in a few days. We've got medicine." Griffy paused, waiting for a response. The line remained quiet. "The lake will be open soon," he continued. "The DNR ranger in charge is the best. And you wouldn't be in the way. Uncle Dell always needs help."

"No, no," his dad finally replied. "It's not going to work out this time. Maybe another year."

*Year?* Griffy's mind screamed and then frantically searched for a better solution.

"Well, you can come up another week, right? Everything will be back to normal in a few weeks."

"It's not going to happen this summer."

"But I learned to fillet. I can drive *The Lucky 13*. I can—"

"End of discussion, son. Let's not make this worse, okay? Put Dell back on, and you get yourself well."

Griffy had let the phone drop from his ear as his dad continued talking. He was saying something about enjoying the rest of the summer, but Griffy didn't hear it. He had handed the phone to Uncle Dell and silently walked away.

Still under the lake's hypnotic spell, Griffy sighed woefully. His mom had been right. She had warned him not to get his hopes up about his dad, but he hadn't listened. Tears slowly welled in his eyes, as he remembered the lessons Pike had given him just weeks earlier. *All for my dad. How stupid of me.* He didn't bother to fight back the tears; he just let them build. Those tears brought him to bad thing number three: Rick. His mom knew only too well how disappointed and upset Griffy was, so she had sent her boyfriend to the rescue. *Great plan, Mom. Way to go on that one.* He barely noticed as a tear rolled down his face, to his chin, and finally into his palms. Okay, so Rick was helping Uncle Dell. That much Griffy would admit. But he was annoying Griffy—big time. Griffy didn't want Rick around, period. Luckily, Rick and Uncle Dell spent a lot of their time on the phone relocating Whispering Pines guests. Many guests still wanted a vacation up north—just not on Lost Land Lake. Uncle Dell had lost more than a week's worth of reservations so far, and more cancellations were coming in every day. His uncle and Rick tried to convince panicked guests that the snakehead invasion had been greatly exaggerated. When that didn't work—and it rarely did—they switched to customer service mode and offered guests the opportunity to change their reservation to Empire Lodge over on Spider Lake. That resort had plenty of vacancies and had offered to accommodate any Lost Land Lake vacationers.

Unfortunately, Rick took some long breaks from phone duty every day, and it was during these breaks that Griffy tried desperately to avoid him. But it was totally useless. The guy wouldn't go away. He always wanted to do something: "Let's go hike the snowmobile trails." "Let's go to the quarry and do some target practice." "Let's go check out the Ojibwe Indian reservation." "Let's go explore the abandoned Boy Scout camp." And Pike was always game for whatever Rick came up with. *Traitor,* Griffy grumbled. It was difficult to refuse to go, with Pike doing a happy dance right next to him. Rick had been at Whispering Pines less than a week, and Griffy was more than ready to see him go. Why couldn't it have been his dad here? Why couldn't he—

Spinner suddenly jumped up, startling Griffy from his thoughts. The lake waters slowly came back into focus, and he heard voices approaching from behind him. Spinner bolted toward the sound. As his mind returned to the present, Griffy realized his face and his butt were wet. How long had he been sitting here? He must have been crying at some point, and the damp, sandy ground had soaked through his jeans.

"Yo, Grif," Pike called. "Let's move it. Get off your rear."

Griffy hurriedly wiped his face dry before he turned around. He and Pike, with Gil as their driver, were supposed to take a load of garbage and miscellaneous junk to the old dump this afternoon. Since the resort was empty, Dell had had the boys organizing and de-cluttering the outbuildings and grounds all week.

Pike got one look at Griffy's puffy red face and stopped short. "Whoa. *Dude.* What's up?" His face contorted in puzzlement, as he took a hesitant step backward.

"What's up, you moron, is that his dad isn't here," Gil announced and shoved her brother as she walked by him and toward Griffy. She came over and sat down, and Spinner followed her. "Your dad's got his own issues," she said to Griffy. She spoke soft and low, with real concern in her voice. Griffy was taken aback by her kindness and attention. She had had very little to do with the boys this summer. She had had better things to do, like cruising around in her beat-up truck. "None of it has anything to do with you," Gil continued. "Don't let him ruin the rest of your summer. He's the one missing out, not you."

"Yeah," Pike chimed in. "And that Rick guy's pretty cool. Look at all the fun stuff we've been doing witho—"

Gil picked up a rock and threw it at her brother. It popped him in the knee.

"Owwwww! Hey, watch it! That's the muskie leg."

Gil made a throat-slicing motion with her hand and shot Pike a look that could kill. Spinner stood up and barked at him.

"What?" Pike questioned. "Why are you all looking at me like that? What did I do now? I just stated the facts. What's wrong with that?"

Gil's eyes looked to the sky, as she slowly shook her head. "Subtlety is not your strong suit. That's for sure."

Pike threw his arms in the air. "Sweet Brie. Grif, help me here."

Strangely, their bickering got to Griffy—in a good way—and a reluctant smile inched its way across his face. He stood up, brushing sand and pine needles off his rear end. Gil followed his lead.

"It's all good, you two. Thanks. I'm fine now. A little pity party, that's all." He walked up to Pike and punched him in the arm. "But I really don't want to hear about your buddy Rick any more."

"My buddy?" Pike snorted. "Oh, come on. He's not—"

Gil punched him in the other arm. "Enough, already."

Pike looked to Griffy, then to Gil. He reluctantly nodded. "Okay. Okay. No more Rick. Sorry. But I still don't think he's a bad guy."

Gil and Griffy rolled their eyes at each other, just as Rick appeared in the distance. The man waved and jogged toward them.

"Right on cue," Griffy muttered sarcastically.

"There you guys are," Rick said through panting breaths. "I've been looking for you. I found that potato launcher over in the garage. Dell told me all about it," he chuckled.

Gil shot him an annoyed look. "It really wasn't funny."

"No, no, of course not." Rick elbowed Griffy in the side and smiled. Griffy didn't respond. Pike looked at the ground and fidgeted. Awkward silence followed.

"Well, anyway," Rick pushed on. "I made another one, so you boys wouldn't have to share. Got a nice supply of hair spray going, too." He looked to Gil. "I can make you one, if you want."

She quickly shook her head and waved him off. "That's okay, really."

"Well, at least come check it out," he urged. "All of you. Come on." He took a few steps back, coaxing them with a gesture toward the other side of the peninsula.

The three kids just stood there. No one made a move. Griffy could feel tension building around them. Pike looked at him, then at Gil, then at Rick, then back to Griffy. Griffy glared a don't-you-dare look at him.

"Oh, come on, you guys." Pike finally whined. "Let's go shoot the potato launcher. This is nuts."

"We can't," Gil reminded him. "We've got to go to the dump." She looked at Rick. "Sorry."

"Oh," he brushed off her excuse, "that can wait."

"Yeah," Pike agreed, "that can wait."

Griffy stared blankly into Rick's pleading face. *He's not going to take no for an answer. No way, Jose.*

"Come on," Rick coaxed again. "I'll go to the dump and help you."

Pike clasped his hands together and turned to Griffy. "He'll help us," he begged.

Now Griffy stared blankly into his friend's pleading face. Pike moved his eyebrows up and down, nodded, and smiled enticingly at him. That goofy look always made Griffy laugh, so he locked his lips together and tried hard to stifle the laughter. His eyes began to water, and his face turned red. Suddenly, air exploded out of his nose and sprayed wet mucous all over Pike.

"You're both so gross," Gil groaned as her brother and Griffy wiped the discharge from their faces.

"I'm going to take that as a yes," Pike announced, and both boys burst into laughter.

Rick seized the opportunity. "Don't move," he ordered. "I can bring everything over here." He gave them a confirming nod and then took off jogging across the peninsula. Within minutes, they saw Rick awkwardly juggling a potato launcher, potatoes, a ramrod, and a can of aerosol hair spray as he half walked, half jogged back to them.

Pike grabbed Griffy by the arm and dragged him along, as he ran up to meet the man. Both boys relieved Rick of a few items.

"Thanks," he said and readjusted the remaining objects as he walked. "Let's get this show on the road."

Back on the banks of Whispering Pines Bay, the four organized their equipment and prepared for launch. Griffy and Pike examined the weapon Rick had made. It was a little shorter—by about a foot, Griffy guessed—than the one Mr. Hanover had given them, was made of white plumbing pipe, and had a red ignition button. The end of the barrel unscrewed to expose the ignition chamber.

"Everyone ready?" Rick asked. "Who's first?"

Gil, showing the first sign of interest in the activity, raised her hand. "Me. I'll go." She turned to the boys. "Load it up for me."

When the launcher was ready, they handed it over. She aimed high in the sky over Whispering Pines Bay.

"When you're ready," Rick instructed, "just push the button, there. Hold it tight. There shouldn't be any kickback, but I'm not sure." He smiled encouragingly.

Gil shot him a skeptical look as she announced: "Test launch number one. Ready, aim, FIRE!" The potato shot into the late afternoon sky with a loud *whoooosh* and then fell in an arc into the bay water. Everyone cheered. Spinner ran up and down the bank, barking out at the lake.

The sixteen-year-old nodded her approval. "Okay. That was cool." She shrugged dismissively and handed the device to Rick.

He beamed proudly and passed the launcher to Griffy. "You're up."

Griffy hesitated before taking the object. He really didn't want to participate, but Rick looked so happy, he couldn't refuse him. Pike loaded the gun, and Griffy filled the ignition chamber with hair spray. He aimed straight across the lake and fired. As the potato blasted out of the barrel, Griffy felt heat on his forearm. For just a second, it felt as if a hair dryer had blown warm air across his arm. Cheers broke out around him as the others followed the vegetable's trajectory. Griffy didn't watch, but instead lowered the launcher and took a look at his arm. A raw red patch had popped up there, stretching across his white forearm in a large rectangle.

Rick gave Griffy a congratulatory pat on the back, and then he noticed the red mark. "What's that?" he asked and took the boy's arm. His face quickly darkened. "What happened?"

Griffy looked up at him. "I don't know. But it doesn't hurt. I don't feel anything."

Gil and Pike stepped up for a look. "Oh wow," Pike gasped. "That's wicked."

"No, that's bad," Gil corrected. "Very bad."

Rick examined the launcher. He adjusted his eyeglasses and sighed heavily. "There's a hole in the ignition chamber." He pointed at it and handed it over to Pike. "The caulk came loose."

Pike nodded. "So the flames shot out."

"And fried my arm," Griffy finished.

"Yep," Rick replied and took the boy's arm again. "I'm so sorry." He shook his head sadly. The man looked miserable.

"It doesn't hurt, just looks bad," Griffy repeated. "I'm fine, really."

Rick kept shaking his head. "That looks like a third-degree

burn to me. You've got no skin left. We better get Dell and get you to the hospital. Your mom is going to kill me."

Griffy suppressed a smile as he slowly nodded his okay. *Kill you?* he was thinking. *Really? Finally, some good news.*

# THE EMERGENCY
# ROOM

Rick tapped the buttons on a vending machine at the Minong Clinic as Dell walked up beside him. A cup dropped down and steaming coffee started to pour into it. He glanced sadly over at Dell and then turned back to the machine.

"He'll come around," Dell said. "Don't worry."

Rick sighed long and heavily. "I don't think so." He reached for the coffee cup and offered it to Dell, who signaled, "No thanks." As Rick sipped from the cup, he stared at Griffy, who was seated a few yards away. "I've tried everything. The kid wants nothing to do with me." He motioned toward the boy. "Now, I've burned him, probably scarred him for life. He's got to hate me."

"Oh, I don't know about that," Dell said. "Look at him." Griffy was showing off the burn to a young girl, as Pike and Gil enthusiastically told the story behind the injury. The girl listened and looked in awe at the three older kids. "He's enjoying this. That scar will be a badge of honor. He and Pike will be talking about this for days."

Rick shrugged. "Maybe."

A nurse, studying a clipboard as she walked, entered the clinic lobby. "Corbett Griffith," she announced, then looked up and scanned the room. Her expressionless face quickly changed to surprise when she saw Pike and Griffy. "Not you two again."

The boys beamed at her. "Yep, us again," Pike chirped.

"Let's see." She tapped a finger on her cheek. "We've had a knife wound, intestinal flukes … now what?"

"A burn," Griffy said and held out his arm.

"Well, I'd say so." She pulled a pair of latex gloves out of her pocket, put them on, and carefully took his arm.

"It didn't hurt at all," Griffy boasted. "Still doesn't."

She smiled. "The burn's pretty deep. You probably killed all the nerves there." She twisted his arm gently this way and that as she spoke. "That's why it doesn't hurt. No nerves, no feeling." She grinned. "You'll have to tell me how you did this once we get in the examination room." She looked around until she spotted Dell. She motioned to him. "You can come on back."

"Can I come? Can I come?" Pike pleaded.

The nurse smiled again. "That's up to Corbett." She looked to the boy for an answer.

"It's Griffy, and, sure, he can come."

"Right. Griffy. Sorry." She turned to Dell. "This won't take long. Doctor's probably just going to bandage it up."

"All right. That's fine," he said; then he gave Rick a knowing glance. "We'll stay out here and start on the paper work. Gil?"

The teen's head shot up at the sound of her name. "Huh?"

She had been looking over the young girl's injury: a smashed thumb.

"Go in with the boys, will you?"

"Sure," she answered and shrugged in that cool, casual teenage way. "Whatever."

The nurse waved them forward, and the three followed her into the examination room. She escorted them to one of four bays separated by thick blue curtains that dropped from a rail along the ceiling down to the tiled floor. She grabbed the side of the curtain and pulled. "The doctor will want to take a look first," she said as the curtain sailed around them. "It'll just be a few minutes. Sit tight." Then she disappeared behind the billowy blue wall.

About ten minutes later, the doctor popped in, verified that Griffy had a third-degree burn, gave the nurse some instructions, and left. Griffy sat on the exam table, swinging his legs back and forth, joking around with Pike and Gil, as they waited for the nurse to return once again. They didn't have to wait long before she entered, carrying a tray of gauze, tape, scissors, and cream. She chuckled as she placed the tray on the table next to Griffy. "A guy just came in with a fish bite, a bad one. We get a lot of fishing accidents, but not many fish bites." She took Griffy's left arm. "I'll have to get the story on that one, too." She paused. "Speaking of stories, what happened there?" She pointed to a thin five-inch-long scar running down the boy's arm.

"Fish attack," Pike boasted. "He saved my life."

"Really?" The nurse looked Griffy curiously in the eye. "So, you're a hero, huh?" Griffy's face flushed red, and he nodded shyly. She smiled and went to work on the burn, rubbing it with cream and covering it with gauze. "We don't get many fish attacks either," she continued. "You must be the boys who hauled in that killer muskie a few years ago."

Griffy sat a little taller. "We are," he bragged.

"Ahem," Gil coughed into her hand and stepped forward. "Excuse me. That's boys and *girl*!" She pointed to herself. "I helped save him, too—and bring in that muskie."

"Yeah, yeah." Pike waved his sister back. "Whatever. You don't bear the scars." He lifted the leg of his shorts, revealing his own scar. "Top that."

Gil scowled and took a step back.

The nurse nodded. "That is some battle scar. I can understand a muskie attack. Everyone wants to catch one of those. But this guy," she pointed to the next exam room, "said he was attacked by a dogfish." Griffy's head shot up. Pike and Gil moved closer. "Wouldn't you just cut the line and let it go?" the nurse questioned. "Why mess with it?" All three opened their mouths to answer, but she didn't give them a chance. Instead, she went into nurse mode. "Okay, you're going to need to keep the wound dry and covered, and put this medicated cream on it twice a day." She looked each kid in the eye. "You'll need to schedule a follow-up in about a week. Got it?" They all nodded. "I need to get you a prescription for the cream. Stay right here." With that, she disappeared behind the curtain again.

As soon as she'd left, Griffy anxiously turned to Pike and Gil. "You don't think?" he asked.

"Nawwwww," Pike answered. "Couldn't be."

"Sure, it could," Gil countered. "I mean, I've never even seen a dogfish, and now they're popping up everywhere. So, yes, it could be." She bit her lip and exhaled. "I wonder what lake that guy's on?"

Suddenly the exam room next door came alive. "Those dang fish are crazy!" a man exclaimed, as the curtain rustled with movement. "All I did was stick my arm in the water. That's it. And the thing attacked! Never seen anything like it."

"Hop up on the table here, and let's have a look," a nurse instructed.

A third person entered the makeshift room. The curtain whooshed as it was pulled shut. "Wow. A dogfish did this? What size?"

"About an eight-pounder," the injured man answered.

"You're kidding me! Where did you catch it?"

"I didn't catch it. No, no. I'm keeping it for the DNR. I have a fishery. Don't know what she's doing with them, but this is the second batch I've had. First ones were small but still ornery, nasty things. The two I've got now are vicious monsters."

"I'll say," the nurse agreed. "Tore your hand wide open."

"You know it. They've even bit the DNR ranger. Right on her arm!"

"No kidding? Well, you're going to need stitches, maybe a butterfly bandage to close that up," the other nurse stated. "We'll get the doctor."

As the room next door went quiet, the kids looked at each other in disbelief.

"Those fish have to be snakeheads," Gil whispered.

"But the DNR?" Pike questioned in a hushed voice. "They wouldn't be involved. Would they?"

"No," Griffy answered, matching Pike's quiet tone. His face filled with confusion. "And who's the *she* he was talking about?"

The others shrugged. Gil's eyes slowly narrowed. "Well, I want to know who the *he* is." She straightened her shoulders resolutely, walked to where the curtain met the wall, and cautiously peeked through to the other side. Then, in one quick movement, she pulled the curtain aside.

"Gil," the boys admonished in hushed voices. "You can't—"

"Hey, Mr. Dooley," she greeted the man, hand still clasped on the curtain, then looked back over her shoulder at the boys. "It's okay. I know him." The teen summoned them with a quick nod. "Come on." Then she disappeared into the other room.

Griffy hopped off the exam table, and he and Pike hustled quickly through the curtain after her. Mr. Dooley jumped a little and jerked his head left and right, as the kids entered. "What? Where?" He looked over both shoulders as if searching for help. "What? Well ... you shouldn't be in here," he finally announced and eyed the three cautiously.

"Oh, it's okay," Gil assured him. "Griffy's here for a burn." She pointed to the boy's bandaged arm.

Mr. Dooley's eyes darted over to Griffy, then back to Gil. "I still don't think you should be in here. Go on back to your own side, now—you hear me?"

Gil ignored the demand. "Mr. Dooley, could the fish that bit you be one of those snakeheads?"

"One what?"

Impatience filled her voice as she spoke each word slowly and clearly. "Northern. Snakehead."

Griffy saw no recognition in the old man's face. "That invasive species from Asia," he explained. "They look very similar to dogfish."

"I don't know what you're talking about," the man huffed.

With a towel pressed to his injured hand, he lifted both arms off his lap and motioned to the curtain with them. "Leave me be, and get on back to your own room."

Pike looked in astonishment at the old man. "You mean you've never heard of it?"

"It's been all over the *Minong Ledger* for weeks," Gil said. "Front page."

"Yeah," Griffy continued. "The DNR closed Lost Land Lake because of them."

"What?" the man questioned sharply. "They did what?"

Gil raised her in eyebrows in exasperation. "Don't you read the paper?"

"No, I don't take the paper," he snapped. "Nothing going on in the world that interests me."

"Well, this has got to," Griffy pleaded. "Lost Land Lake is really hurting now. Someone released three snakeheads in the lake."

"We don't know who. We don't know why," Pike went on. "But Whispering Pines Lodge and The Happy Hooker are losing business because of it."

Mr. Dooley turned his head to Gil, showing the first signs of interest. "Losing business?" he asked.

Gil pounced. "Yes. We lose business. You lose business."

The man dropped his head and stared at his injury for a moment. The three kids fidgeted anxiously. "I thought it was DNR business," he finally said. Mr. Dooley looked up. "I also thought it was suspicious. Those fish were shipped to me from Chicago, and there were four—in the first batch."

"Four?" Griffy blurted out.

Mr. Dooley nodded.

"You mentioned a *she*." Gil spoke hurriedly. "Who's the *she*?"

Mr. Dooley delayed his answer with a long, slow exhale. "That DNR ranger. Oh, what's her name?" He snapped his fingers a couple times as he thought. "J—"

"Jo?" the kids exclaimed in unison and exchanged stunned looks.

"That's it." He paused. "I can't believe she would ever do anything to harm one of the lakes."

"Me neither," Griffy agreed. "She wouldn't."

Pike grunted his disapproval. "No way."

Gil spun around to face them, palms held out in front of her. "Whoa. Slow down," she ordered. "We can't just ignore all this. Maybe we should go to the fishery and check these fish out first."

Mr. Dooley exhaled again. "That's just it," he said. "I was packing them up for her when that pit bull of a fish attacked me. She picked them up about an hour ago. Wherever she was going, she's most likely there by now."

"Oh no," the teen groaned. She turned to the boys. Gil's mind was obviously working in overdrive, Griffy thought. She had an *aha*, all-circuits-firing kind of look on her face. She grabbed his arm. "We've got to go."

"Hey!" he whined. "Watch the burn."

"Oh, man up and come on," she ordered and yanked both boys out of Mr. Dooley's exam room. "We might be too late already."

Both boys pulled out of her grip and stood dumbfounded just outside the curtain. Griffy wasn't quite sure what was going on or why Gil was in such a panic. And by the look on Pike's face, his friend wasn't so sure, either.

"Don't just stand there. Let's go," Gil barked impatiently and gave her brother a shove from behind. She grabbed Griffy's arm again, pulling him as she scooted Pike forward.

"What's wrong with you?" her brother questioned. "Jo? Seriously? You think it's Jo?"

"There's no time for questions. I'll explain in the car. Just trust me." With that, she shepherded the boys toward the lobby door.

"Hey! Hey! Wait," the nurse called after them, waving a piece of paper in the air. "You forgot the prescription."

Gil raced back to her and snatched the piece of paper. "Thank you," she called as she ran back to Pike and Griffy, and then they were out the lobby door.

# CAUGHT
# IN THE ACT

The SUV sped along County A highway, following its twists and turns and rolling over its sloping hills, as nausea swept over Griffy. He sat in the backseat, hunched over, hugging his cramping midsection. The boy wasn't sure whether his symptoms were caused by the roller coaster ride back to Whispering Pines, by the parasite still living in his intestines, or by the fact that yet another adult—one he should have been able to trust—might have deceived him.

First and foremost, there was his dad. A dad should always be there for you, but his wasn't. When it came to his dad, Griffy was now sure of only one thing: the man would back out on him.

Then there was Doctor Potts, the University of Wisconsin archaeologist from last summer. An archaeologist should dig and fight for the truth, but this one hadn't. This one had lied to

Griffy's face and tried to reap the rewards of a discovery that wasn't his.

Now there was Jo, the DNR ranger. She had been around during the Master Fisherman Muskie Competition, and she had been there to stop Doctor Potts. Could she really be trying to ruin Lost Land Lake? Griffy went over Gil's theory as the SUV pulled into the Whispering Pines drive. Jo was a DNR ranger, so she had knowledge of invasive species and unlimited access to Lost Land Lake. *All true.* Mr. Dooley said the snakeheads had bitten a DNR ranger. Jo had a bandage on her arm at the meeting with Matt Mullen. *Gil and I both saw it.* Jo's family owned Empire Lodge, and that resort was in financial trouble. Griffy hadn't known Jo was connected with Empire Lodge, but he did know that this resort was handling all of their cancellations. *Could be a motive.* And, lastly, Mr. Dooley had snakeheads and said he had gotten them from Jo. *The smoking gun, but still ...*

Gil's door suddenly flew open, and Griffy watched her jump out of the vehicle before it came to a complete stop. "What's our plan of attack?" she asked, eagerly bouncing up and down in the drive.

"Just hold up," Uncle Dell calmly commanded with one leg in and one leg out of the driver's seat. "There will be no attack. We all heard your theory, but it just doesn't sit well." Gil pursed her lips together. She looked ready for a fight, but Dell held up his hand. "We'll take a few boats out, okay? Look around. No harm in that." Gil's face softened as Dell summoned the boys. "You two take out *The Lucky 13*. And no funny business out there," he ordered. Pike saluted. Griffy gave a nod. Dell turned back to Gil. "Go down to Sleepy Eye, but don't stir any trouble up down there. Just get Danny and get a pontoon." She signaled thumbs-up and ran to her pickup truck. Dell continued, "Rick, take one of the cabin boats out. I'll go track down Mullen, just in case. He's probably at Looney's Landing."

The group broke from their huddle, like basketball players, and moved into position: Dell toward the lodge, Rick toward Whispering Pines Bay, and the boys across the peninsula.

"I'll drive," Pike announced as he and Griffy ran up to *The Lucky 13*, which rested on shore in the swim bay.

"Fine by me," Griffy said. "I'll take anchor duty."

As Pike seated himself at the motor, Griffy unwrapped the anchor's rope from around a nearby tree and placed it in the boat. He grabbed both sides of the bow, pushed the boat away from the sandy shore, and hopped in. In no time, Pike had the motor fired up, and the two zoomed past the swim raft and out into Lost Land Lake. The early evening sun glowed across the water, and Griffy squinted against it as he scanned the lake. Nothing. The last of the electro-fishing boats would have left a few hours earlier, and the lake was still closed. He turned to Pike and pointed left. "Let's follow the shoreline," he yelled over the buzz of the motor. If Jo wasn't out on the water, maybe she was hiding somewhere in the forest that surrounded Lost Land Lake.

"Aye, aye," Pike called back.

Warm air blew through Griffy's hair and water sprayed his face as they searched the shore near The Happy Hooker, Looney's Landing, and then Sunken Island Resort. Still they saw nothing. As they neared Ted Hanover's place, the wind picked up, and Griffy heard the echo of a dog's agitated barking. Was that Mr. Hanover's puppy? He leaned forward and was searching the shore more closely, when *The Lucky 13* took a sudden sharp turn to the right. He slid across its worn bench and into the boat's side. "Hey!"

Griffy yelled as he gripped the rim to steady himself. He looked over his shoulder. "What are yo—" He stopped midsentence and followed Pike's punctuated pointing, as *The Lucky 13* bumped across a mass of growing waves. A pontoon and a motorboat sat on the outskirts of Shallow Pass, just off Big Crooked Creek. As the small boat fought the foaming waves, Griffy could see Gil struggling to steer the pontoon and Danny Rubedieux leaning dangerously over its gated edge. A dog ran back and forth across the pontoon's outer platform, barking fiercely. *Spinner! Where'd he come from?* The setting sun cast shadows on the site, and Griffy couldn't see anyone in the seesawing motorboat.

As they entered Shallow Pass, Pike slowed *The Lucky 13*. Griffy could now hear Gil barking orders toward the eighteen-foot motorboat, while pleading with Danny, the blind owner of Sleepy Eye Rentals, to be careful. Griffy's eyes darted over the scene and locked on a dark figure crouched down and leaning over the side of the fiberglass motorboat. A hooded sweatshirt covered the person's face, as he or she held something over the side. *Could that be Jo?* Griffy strained to see, but the person never looked up. Instead, he or she stayed low as if hiding.

"Finally!" Gil cried when she spied *The Lucky 13*. "Hurry!" she called to the boys. "We think it's a snakehead." She pointed downward. The person in the motorboat was intently pushing a large fish back and forth in the water. The hooded figure's head jerked nervously side to side as the boats converged on the site.

"Gil, get us closer," Danny begged.

"I'm trying, I'm trying," the teen complained. "The boat's too big." A gust of wind dragged the scarf holding back her long hair. She grabbed it before it could fly off. "The wind is getting too strong," she cried.

"Drop anchor, then," the young man ordered. He moved away from the gate and listened as *The Lucky 13* inched closer. The wind whipped his shoulder-length blond hair around as he waved the boys over. "Get to the other side, quick," he instructed. "That fish is in shock. It won't swim—for now."

Pike circled the dinghy around, and Griffy reached down for a net lying under his bench.

"Get ready, Grif," Pike called to his friend.

The boys' small wooden boat gave a wide berth to the much larger boat's anchor line and then easily pulled to within a few feet of the hooded person still crouched over the water. Griffy readied the net, but just as he was about to lower it into the lake, the hooded figure looked up. Griffy tried to make out the shadowy face before him. The two locked eyes just as the hooded shape grabbed his net and pulled. The handle slipped from Griffy's grip.

Pike snorted, "I don't think so," and slammed the motor into reverse.

Griffy swayed off balance, and his hands instinctively tightened on the net.

"Hold on, Grif!" Pike warned.

As the boat sped away, Griffy careened backwards, falling hard onto the wooden bench behind him. The net was ripped out of the hooded figure's hands.

"Ha—take that!" Pike yelled triumphantly.

Spinner's alarmed barks filled the air.

"The fish!" Gil exclaimed. "It's loose." The beam of a large flashlight lit up the water as she scanned the area. "I don't see it!"

Griffy signaled with his hand for Pike to stop. "Bring us

back," he commanded and urgently waved the small boat forward. But before Pike could switch gears, Spinner charged down the pontoon's platform and hit the water at a run.

"Holy chedda cheese," Pike marveled. "Look at him go."

"No, Spinner, no," his sister called after the dog. She quickly followed Spinner's path with her flashlight. A few feet away from its beam, Griffy spied a large fish floating on its side. It flipped itself upright, struggled to swim for a few seconds, and then rolled sideways again. Spinner paddled faster. The building waves knocked the dog left and right. He pounced on the snakehead just as a wave crashed downward, forcing the dog and fish underwater. Gil shrieked. Griffy gasped and held his breath, until Spinner popped back up with the fish locked between his jaws. The boys and Gil cheered.

"Good job," Danny praised, then whistled and called, "Come on, boy." Spinner turned and, struggling to hold the fish above water, paddled back toward the pontoon. Danny kneeled over the platform's edge ready to retrieve the dog. Gil joined him. "Come on, Spinner," she encouraged. "You can do it."

The hum of an approaching boat motor startled Griffy, and he whipped his head around to see Rick, in one of the Whispering Pines boats. "Hey, you! Stop right there!" the man bellowed as he closed in on the scene.

With Spinner struggling in the water, no one had watched the mysterious hooded figure, who was now wrestling with a large container, hoisting it up and over the rocking boat's side. Pike turned *The Lucky 13* and gunned it, as Griffy watched a fish slide to the container's edge, hang there, and then slide back inside.

"Hurry," Griffy urged his friend. "She's got another one."

Griffy readied the net, but they weren't close enough, and

he knew one more shake would put that fish in the water. They didn't have much time. They needed Matt Mullen. They needed help. They needed—

Whoooomp!

A blast echoed across the lake, and a bright flash filled the evening sky. Griffy's eyes shot to the source of the blue-and-orange flames. *Rick! Holy chedda cheese! He has a potato launcher. Why didn't we think of that?* Within seconds, a large potato slammed into the hooded figure's midsection, spraying chunks at the approaching *Lucky 13*. As the figure doubled over, the container crashed down on the boat's rim, and in a burst of water, the fish inside flew out. Griffy threw himself across the bow. With the net stretched out before him, he snagged the snakehead by the tail as it dropped from the sky. The animal teetered on the net's rim, threatening to escape into the lake at any moment. Griffy did the only thing he could think of. With his last bit of strength, he flicked the net like a frying pan. The snakehead flipped up in the air and fell into the net. Thump! Its weight pulled Griffy farther out of the boat. He couldn't find the strength to pull back up. His bandaged arm throbbed. His muscles burned and twitched. The net dipped lower and lower.

"Hang on, Griffy," Gil encouraged from the pontoon. "Don't let him drop."

Danny cheered like a sideline coach: "You got this! You got this!"

Griffy wasn't so sure. He tried to pull back again, but in his awkward position he didn't have the power or the leverage. The net slipped, and water engulfed the fish. It flipped and twisted angrily, trying to escape. Its mouthful of thorny teeth tore at the cotton netting. *Sweet Brie!* Griffy's mind cried. *It's going to gnaw its way to freedom!* He took a deep, determined breath. "I got this," he said.

"No," Pike countered, coming up behind his friend. "*We* got this."

He grabbed Griffy by the life jacket, and both boys heaved with all their might. Griffy, the net, the snakehead, and Pike careened backward, landing inside the boat with a thud.

"Thanks, man," Griffy sighed in relief. The snakehead, bound and tangled in the netting, twitched helplessly on his stomach.

"No problem. Now, get off," Pike grumbled from the bottom of the pile.

Griffy chuckled as he hoisted himself onto a bench and quickly pushed the netted snakehead underneath it. He turned around and was taken aback to see Rick holding *The Lucky 13* steady while idling the motor of his own boat. His mother's boyfriend had been there to help him, not once, but twice. *Maybe the guy was okay. Maybe ...*

"You all right?" Rick asked.

Griffy nodded. He awkwardly cleared his throat. "That was a great shot. Thanks."

"Any time," Rick said and smiled brightly.

Pike adjusted his T-shirt and shorts, as he scrambled into his position at the motor. He looked around. "Where's Jo? Is she okay?"

Rick pointed to a dark shape hunched over in the motorboat. "Out cold, I think." He made a diving motion with his arm.

Pike snickered. "You beaned her good."

"Hey," Griffy interjected. "We don't know for sure it's Jo."

"Who else would it be?" Pike countered. Griffy slumped. Pike was right. Who else would it be?

Sirens suddenly filled the air, and Rick motioned toward a small fleet of DNR boats speeding across the lake. "Calvary's coming. Let's let them deal with that."

Spinner barked urgently from the pontoon, and Rick signaled to Gil. *The Lucky 13*, the Whispering Pines boat, and the Sleepy Eye pontoon slowly moved back to give the DNR some room.

A few minutes later, rangers had the area surrounded. Spotlights lit up the motorboat as Matt Mullen's voice barked orders over a bullhorn. He boarded the boat and helped the dark figure stand up. "She's okay," he told his crew. "But let's get her to the clinic ASAP." As he escorted the culprit off the boat, the hood hiding her face slipped back, and dark-blonde hair spilled out. Griffy's heart sank. It *was* Jo. The woman glanced over her shoulder as she stepped onto the DNR boat. Griffy saw her face for the first time that evening. He leaped up, and his mouth dropped open. "That's not Jo," he blurted for all to hear.

"Of course it's not," a woman shouted from a nearby DNR boat.

Pike and Griffy turned toward the voice. The woman stepped out of the shadows and into the beam of a spotlight. It was DNR ranger Jo Patterson.

Pike leaped to his feet, too, and looked from boat to boat. He pointed at the now-hoodless woman. "Hey, that's not Jo," he announced. He pointed again. "That is." He then turned to Griffy and loudly lectured. "I told you it couldn't be Jo, but you wouldn't listen."

"What?" Griffy shot back and spun to confront his friend. "You did no—" Griffy stopped midsentence when he saw the playful grin covering Pike's face. His eyes narrowed. "Whatever."

# MOTIVES AND MISTAKES

A few days after the heroic snakehead capture, Griffy sipped on the straw of a "suicide" fountain drink as he walked along a pine-paneled wall at Looney's Landing. He had never been inside the bar and restaurant and was mesmerized by the décor of the place. When he and Pike had first entered, they'd made a beeline for the soda fountain. Since it was way too difficult to choose from all the syrup selections, the boys had gone with a squirt of each. Then and only then did Griffy turn his attention to the bright neon signs and mounted fish that hung everywhere. Some of the signs appeared to move in waves. Others slowly changed scenes. In one, he saw a team of Clydesdales pulling a red wagon round and round a snowy scene.

Griffy watched his friend jog across the room as he sipped from his own drink. Pike didn't remove his lips from the straw and didn't say a word as he stopped in front of Griffy. The boy just held out his fist and opened it. He had quarters. Still slurping from his straw, Griffy nodded and grinned. "Nice."

A series of small glass display cases lined the pine wall at Looney's Landing. The cases resembled hanging pictures, complete with carved frames. Inside each case, comically dressed stuffed squirrels and chipmunks played cards, hunted, fished, and skied against painted backgrounds. A couple of the cases had quarter slots, and Griffy couldn't wait to see what would happen as Pike put a quarter in. The boys pointed and chuckled as the animals jerked to life. Some sped down ski slopes. Others twirled on ice skates. Still others trudged through the snow-packed ground on cross-country skis.

Uncle Dell didn't think Looney's Landing was an appropriate place for a kid. That's why Griffy had never been here, but the twelve-year-old didn't see what was so wrong with the place. Obviously, neither did Matt Mullen. The DNR ranger had invited everyone involved with saving Lost Land Lake out to lunch here. When the waitress had loaded their table with baskets of fish and French fries, Uncle Dell called the boys over. They reluctantly left the picture windows and joined the group that included Danny, Gil, Rick, and Jo.

Mullen raised his glass in a toast. "Here's to Lost Land Lake— its safety and preservation."

Beverage glassed clinked around the table, and conversation broke out among the guests.

With a hurt face, Jo turned to the boys. "So, you really thought I was out to get Lost Land Lake?"

"Not me," Griffy quickly replied.

"Or me," Pike added, then lowered his head. "Well, maybe a little, but Gil ..."

"Okay, okay." His sister held her hands up in defeat. "I was wrong." She looked at Jo and cowered slightly. "Sorry."

"It's all right," Jo assured her with a grin. "I'm glad you three were on top of things. Slightly off the mark, but still on top of things."

"Well, my theory *did* make sense." Gil pouted and planted fists firmly on her hips.

Pike's sister was such a know-it-all that Griffy really wanted to leave her hanging, but he reluctantly agreed: "It did. No one would ever suspect a DNR ranger. It was the perfect cover."

"It was," Jo admitted. "And it was an easy mix-up, especially since my no-good cousin *borrowed*"—she made quotation marks in the air with her fingers to emphasize the word—"one of my ranger uniforms."

"Yep," Pike enthusiastically added, "and releasing the snakeheads right after the electro-fishing wrapped up was brilliant."

"That's right." Her confidence returning, Gil sat up a little straighter. "I knew your family owned the Empire Lodge. I also knew it was in financial trouble. The resort was listed as a short sale in the *Ledger*."

"Huh?" Pike shot his sister a quizzical look. "A short *what*?"

"Sale," Gil answered arrogantly. "Means it was steps away from foreclosure."

"Ooooohhhhhh," her brother moaned sarcastically.

Gil huffed. "I asked Mom, all right?"

"And," Jo quickly jumped in, "Empire Lodge was getting tons of business because of the snakehead invasion."

"Exactly," Gil stated, flicking her finger with an air of triumph.

"Don't forget the bandage," Griffy hurriedly added. "We knew whoever had the snakeheads was bitten by one."

"Yeah," Pike agreed. "Bitten on the arm." He pointed to Jo's still bandaged forearm.

"What happened there?"

"Oh," Jo grinned sheepishly. "It's not a fish bite. I was relocating a bear cub, and it clawed me." She dismissed the injury with a shrug. "So the evidence was there. I'll give you that. But you didn't know one thing. I don't own Empire Lodge, not anymore. When my grandmother died, she left the resort to my cousin, Jody, and me. We are both named after her. Her name was Josephine." She paused. "Anyway, being a DNR ranger is more than a full-time job, so I knew I couldn't handle running a resort. I tried to talk Jody into keeping a couple cabins and selling off the rest. But she wanted the whole resort. I kept one cabin and signed everything else over to her. She resents me to this day for it."

"Then you're the reason she tried to ruin Lost Land Lake. She wanted to get even." Rick joined the conversation.

"Yeah, make you pay," Pike chimed in. He rubbed his hands together in a sinister fashion.

"Something like that." Jo fiddled with her napkin. "I *am* the ranger for Lost Land Lake." She looked around the table. "But in Jody's twisted mind, you all were to blame for her failure."

"How so?" Rick asked.

"Lost Land Lake is a tourism gold mine," Mullen answered. "It's the most profitable and popular lake in the Chequamegon National Forest, largely thanks to you three kids."

"Us?" Gil questioned. "What did we do?"

"How about catching a world record muskie?" Dell replied.

"And discovering a ten-thousand-year-old elk skeleton," Danny added.

Proud grins spread across Pike, Gil, and Griffy's faces.

"So, what happens next?" Danny asked. "What happens to Cousin Jody?"

"Nothing good," Mullen stated matter-of-factly. "She could receive a $250,000 fine and five years in prison. Those last two snakeheads were being tracked by the US Fish and Wildlife Service. We might have been able to handle it all locally, but not now. Now, it's a federal case."

"Tracked?" Griffy asked. "How were they being tracked?"

"With electronic chips," Mullen said. "The feds take this sort of thing very seriously. They confiscate shipments, tag the fish, and track them to their destination."

"A sting operation!" Pike exclaimed.

"Right on," Mullen said. "Our snakeheads first showed up at a live-fish market in Chicago. The feds were on it. I had a voice-mail message waiting the day we brought Jody in."

"Cool," Griffy gushed.

"It gets cooler," Jo said. "The Fish and Wildlife Service will be here tomorrow to start an investigation. A trial of some sort will likely take place in the fall. They'll be talking to everyone involved. That means all of you."

Looks of surprise and shock passed among the lunch guests.

"They're bringing in their own dissection lab," Jo continued. She looked to the three kids. "I bet we could get you guys in to watch a snakehead dissection or two." She raised her eyebrows quizzically at Mullen. He nodded his agreement. "Interested in watching the feds in action?"

"You know it," Pike fired back and elbowed his friend. "We're in. Right, Grif?"

Griffy could hardly spit his words out fast enough. "Oh, yeah. We're in." He looked over at Rick, who had just raised his glass for a drink. "You're in, too—right?"

Rick's eyes popped wide, and he choked on the soda he was swallowing. Uncle Dell clapped him on the back. "You okay, there?" he chuckled, knowingly.

Rick nodded repeatedly before coughing out, "Fine. Fine." He wiped his face with a napkin and cleared his throat. "Wouldn't miss it. Not for the world."

A smile spread across Griffy's face. "Cool."

"So," Uncle Dell announced and raised his glass, "here's to no more snakeheads." Glasses rose to join Dell's, but Mullen quickly waved them down. The lunch guests stared in confusion at him.

"It's not completely over," he explained seriously. "There's one snakehead not accounted for."

"What do you mean?" Dell asked, his glass still hovering over the table.

"Jody released four snakeheads in May," Mullen said. "None of those were tagged. We found three. One is left."

The guests groaned and shifted uneasily in their seats.

Griffy had forgotten about the fourth fish. He bit down on his thumbnail as he brooded. *Wait a minute*, he thought. His mouth flew open. "One can't spawn, so we're good, right?" He looked around the table.

Mullen made a sour face and shook his head. "They can spawn with other fish," he stated. "Create mixed breeds. It's not good. We still need to be on watch."

Griffy's head dropped into his hands. Lost Land Lake was

still in trouble. His eyes met Rick's across the table. The man gave him a reassuring wink and mouthed, "It'll be okay." Griffy halfheartedly smiled back. Everyone around the table sat quietly, and the boy pouted for a moment before lifting his head again. His spirits began to rise. *Rick is right*, he thought. *It will be okay.* Lost Land Lake needed him, and he'd be there for it. They all would. *No question.* Griffy rose from his chair and raised his glass. "Forget snakeheads. Here's to us. The Lost Land Lake …" He hesitated, searching for the right word.

"Alliance," Pike offered as he, too, stood.

"Alliance," Griffy confirmed and started again. "Here's to the Lost Land Lake Alliance. United to protect the lake we love."

"Bring it on," Pike cheered as eight glasses rose in the air and clinked together.

# Epilogue:
# Out on the Lake

A young muskie destined for world record greatness hovered unmoving among the weeds at the bottom of Whispering Pines Bay. It held a strange-looking fish in its sights. The fish wasn't one the young muskie had seen before, and its very presence aroused the predator's urge to attack and to kill. Instinct told the muskie that this strange creature was an enemy, and it knew exactly what the enemy was doing. It was waiting, patiently waiting, for its prey. The enemy's flat, pointy head was stuck just out of the weed bed, and its long feathery fins waved back and forth in the cool water, as a school of crappie swam steadily toward it. The muskie waited, too, its green-gold body and dark vertical bars serving as camouflage against the wall of weeds.

Suddenly, the strange fish lunged forward, but its speed was no match for the powerful muskie. With one thrust of its tail fin, the muskie opened its long snout and engulfed its enemy whole. Before the snakehead could react, its captor's jaws and fanglike teeth had snapped shut around it.

The young muskie, one of Wisconsin's freshwater kings, whipped its tubular body around and disappeared into the depths of Lost Land Lake.

*A special thanks to the students of Danville District 118, whose enthusiasm kept me pushing forward, and to James Moore, Paul Kretekos, and Daniel Stehl.*

Be sure to check out *Muskie Attack* and *Ancient Elk Hunt,*
the first and second books in the *Up North Adventure* series.

www.facebook.com/upnorthadventure

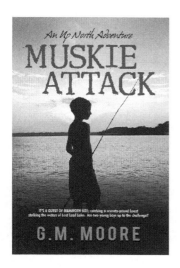

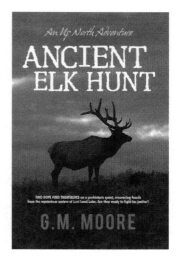

It's a quest of mammoth size:
catching a seventy-pound
beast stalking the waters
of Lost Land Lake. Are two
young boys up to the challenge?

Two boys find themselves on
a prehistoric quest, recovering
fossils from the mysterious
waters of Lost Land Lake. Are
they ready to fight for justice?